$\mathcal{B}$ellydancer

Best wishes

Skghee

Oct 24/94 .

Bellydancer

STORIES

SKY Lee

Press Gang Publishers
Vancouver

"Broken Teeth" was first published in *West Coast Review,* 1981.

The publisher gratefully acknowledges financial assistance from the Canada
Council and the Cultural Services Branch, Province of British Columbia.

Canadian Cataloguing in Publication Data

Lee, Sky.
  Bellydancer

  ISBN 0-88974-039-9

  1. Women – Fiction. I. Title.
PS8573.E353B44 1994   C813'.54   C94-910638-0
PR9199.3.L393B44 1994

Edited by Jamila Ismail and Jennifer Glossop
Design by Val Speidel
Cover photographs by Chick Rice
Author photograph by Bob Hsiang
Typeset in Adobe Garamond
Printed on acid-free paper by Best Gagné Book Manufacturers Inc.
Printed and bound in Canada

Press Gang Publishers
101 - 225 East 17th Avenue
Vancouver, B.C. V5V 1A6
Canada

To Lover

My thanks and best wishes to those who have guided and encouraged me. They are Jamila Ismail, Jim Wong-Chu, Nathan Wong, the late Jacqueline Frewin, Daphne Marlatt, Marlene Enns, Robert Lee, Ginger Lee, Betsy Warland, Marilou Esguerra, Barbara Kuhne, Jennifer Glossop, Cynthia Flood, Saeko Usukawa and Fred Wah.

CONTENTS

Bellydancer

*B*ROKEN TEETH

IT WAS KIND of spring. I stepped off the bus on my way home.
I mean my mother's house on East First Avenue, just off the
freeway. Actually I don't live there. I don't feel a part of it any
more. I didn't grow up in the cold composure that lives there
now. I had other memories, sold off and left behind in a pulp
mill town.

I had qualms about going home to my mother's house. My
mother and a confrontation still lingered there behind a huge
wood-burning stove of long ago. Though nowadays she stuffs a
shiny new electric range with aluminum foil, and she covers the
oven timer with clear Saran Wrap.

But my mother could intimidate me. "Cock! Day after day.
What do you do all the time that you can't even come home, eh?"

How could I even begin to tell my mother about my other
life outside of her house. In fact, I always marched up those
shaky pink back stairs too quickly, with the secret hope that
maybe my mother would not be home. Thus, my token home
visit would be duly recorded and, in turn, reported to her. But
by then I would be sure to be gone. I know she would repeat
the same lines over again, but not to my face.

When I reached the top of the stairs, I banged and clattered
on the screen door. It was locked. I peered through the netting

and the glass, searching beyond the lace curtains for a responsive shadow within. I saw movement and immediately backed away. My eyes dropped to the welcome mat under my feet. Beside the mat, I saw the burned ends of red incense sticks stuck in the smaller half of a small potato. Some ashes dusted the puddle of rainwater that it sat in. The lace curtains lifted and I felt my mother's eyes stare at me. I wondered what special occasion I had missed. All Souls' Day? A Moon Celebration? Maybe the Flower Festival or an Ancestral Birthday. Who knows – maybe even Chinese New Year. I listened to each lock unfasten. The door opened, letting out the cat and her words, "So it's you. After so long, you finally decide to come home." She wanted confrontation. "Cock! Day after day, what have you been up to that you don't even come home, huh?"

"Ah Ma." I was never my mother's match. Already sagging, I repeated dully, "Nothing much." Her eyes bored in. Mine lingered over my task of neatly placing my shoes on the pieces of cardboard boxes she had neatly cut up with a dull bread knife to protect the linoleum. "Any letters come for me?"

"None."

She kept a penetrating glare on me. Suddenly she accused, "Your grandfather died last week."

I was still at the door. But I had never met my grandfather – her father. He lived in Hong Kong. And I was born here. So why accuse me, Mother? Yet, her guilt-ridden blow struck with the desired effect. This man died. This man was supposed to mean something to me. And I didn't even know. I didn't know because I was local born. Because I had moved out. Because I didn't come home to see her. In fact, I still didn't know. But I knew all the implications behind my mother's blunt remark. They flew through the air and imbedded themselves in my skin. I knew these all my life.

Yet I claimed innocence. "Is that so?"

Looking up at her, I noticed a little crocheted flower and a little green fern tip bobby-pinned to black hair. Ornate reading glasses perched on her nose at an acute angle. She softened. I relaxed. My mother was used to my aloofness by now. And that was all the response she would see from me.

"Drink tea?"

"Sure." I sat down at the bright yellow dinette on a matching chair. There were tiny gold flecks in the arborite surface.

My mother put a thick ceramic cup in front of me, coloured like creamed coffee. It had the word Stafford stamped diagonally across its face. Because I was left-handed, the Stafford sign always faced me instead of out when I drank. Years ago, these Stafford-stamped dishes were all the western dishes my parents owned beside the chinese rice bowls and soup spoons painted with wobbly gold fringes and awkward figures. I probably learned to read with the Stafford stamp. My mother said that my father brought them home from the Arlington Hotel where he worked when it changed ownership and name. However, my father said he stole them – one piece at a time, each night when the boss was counting money at the cash register.

"Yep. The old fogey's dead, I guess." My mother was re-steaming some home-made buns in a warped aluminum pot with a burnt black bottom. It danced loudly on the burner as the water inside boiled. I told her I didn't want any if they were filled with sugar and coconut. Pork was OK, though.

"Ah. But he was my father, after all. And your grandfather. How old was he anyway?" She counted on her fingers. "Eighty-nine? He was eighty-nine last November. That's long enough. Your auntie wrote a letter and she said that he had sickened fast, then died fast."

"What did he die from? I asked.

She threw me a look of disgust. "Eat it, I tell you! It's not the coconut-and-sugar kind."

"But it is so!" I complained.

"Well, then, give it to me!" She prodded another steamy bun with her long fingers. "OK. This one is pork."

But it wasn't. I ate it anyway. Across the kitchen, I noticed some plastic flowers that my mother had washed, clinging together and dripping onto a rubber mat beside the sink. They looked cold and seemed to shiver in the vague grey light under the window. Splashed with colour, they tended to make me think that they were real. But I should have known better as my mother talked on and on about a sense of duty. A daughter's duty to her father, something that was foreign to my generation.

"Nothing is valued any more. Nothing is cared for," she said. She softened. "Still, I am only just a daughter."

"Ma," I said, "why are you still buying those cheap plastic flowers?"

"What do you know . . . in the old days . . . the bullying. Back then, women were detested," she hissed, "like animals." Her hands tightened over the fine filigree border of roses around her teacup. "Do you know?"

I said, "They look so gaudy. And you've already got so many, Ma."

"You think it was all stories back in those days, but it was very real . . . "

"They don't look real to me at all." I was annoyed.

"I was eight years old. I was a little girl in the village then. And it was a bright sunny day when the air was fresh and full of wonderful scents. I was very happy. We were on our way to the market to shop – my family and I walked, my father and mother and little brother between them. He was clasping onto their hands, and sometimes they had to drag him. Such a hot day in spring. And the road became so dusty as we approached town.

"Every time we go to town, we always dropped in at third

uncle's house. And who could have known after walking all that way and climbing up all those steep stairs that they would not even stay to drink tea and gossip with the aunties.

"As soon as we came in, my cousin ran up to me and offered to show me new kittens born last night. Excited, he said that the old mother cat had died in her labour. And now, more than likely, her wet little rats of children would not survive long after her. In fact, even as I peered into the dark corner at the back of the kitchen, there was already a limp, still bundle of fur in the quivering mass. Soon I left.

"When I came back into the sitting room, it was deserted. They had gone on without me. Suddenly I heard my mother call shrilly at the top of her voice from the courtyard below. 'You crazy . . . come out here.' Her voice in the distance angry. 'We can't wait out here half a day for her while she sneaks off whenever she pleases.' My old man kept swearing softly to himself, staring at the hard ground. The thought of keeping him waiting out there on the street in the hot sun frightened me. I thought to hurry.

"From the top of the narrow shaky stairwell, I only had eyes for my father's red thunderous face sweating under the glare of the sun; and my mother with a flat expression, fanning him. Near the bottom of the stairs, my little brother was playing. And right in the middle of the second step down, my damned cousin had dropped an orange peel or something. Of course I slipped on it and started falling headlong. What a giddy sensation that was! I jerked back but I still piled face first onto my brother. I was knocked senseless. The jolt almost blacked me out; my head was reeling with pain and shock. I was so sick I retched when I picked myself out of the dust.

"Then I saw my father – and he was a big man – roaring towards me in a tower of rage. Screaming, he was so furious I thought that his face was going to burst open like a melon.

'Damn bitch! Knock over my son, willya. I'll show you.' And my mother. She was shrieking all over the country. 'Sai-la! Sai-la! We're done for. She's killed my son.'

"I knew my old man would beat me to death if he caught me in his fury. But I just sat there, crumpled. Well, he rushed up to me and struck me such a blow across my cheek with his clenched fist. Even then, I was too much in pain to feel it. He grabbed my blouse and dragged me onto my feet. I remember drops of blood soaking into the clean cotton and spotting the dust. His hand raised to strike again.

"This time, by instinct only, I tore myself away like a crazed cat and lunged into the storeroom. I couldn't see through the tears and the turmoil, just threw myself behind the firewood and hid. I didn't know how long I hid there, but my nose and mouth were bleeding like a flood. There was blood all over me – hands, lap, smeared all over the water vats I was sobbing on. Outside, my little brother was yelping loudly, everyone cooing and exclaiming at the same time. My face was torn and so swollen I could hardly breathe. But, worst of all, I had broken and chipped all my front teeth. Some of them just dangled off my shredded gums.

"I had just finished growing them. And, oh, the pain those broken teeth caused me for years afterward! And still my father cursed me. So I crept farther into the woodpile. Later on, when my mother finally rummaged me out of there, her mouth dropped open to see me so bloodied. She said, 'My goodness, look at this thing. She's broken all her teeth.' And to this day, the old bitch still recalls that incident. From time to time, she tells me about it. But I have never forgotten!"

The afternoon light had turned slaty and the leftover tea had grown cold. The re-steamed buns had shrivelled up and hardened again. I sat on my yellow and chrome chair, completely dumbfounded. Yet something in my mother's eyes gleamed as she watched me. So for her satisfaction, I wrinkled up my nose and blurted out a polite "yech." And that was all the response she would see from me. Still, she seemed almost exultant when she whisked her rose teacup and my thick Stafford mug away.

"You know those teeth. They slowly rotted and abcessed. They didn't give me one moment's peace until I came to Canada and got them all pulled out by a dentist here. But I was thirty-four by then. In the old days, there weren't any real dentists in China, you know. Not like here now. People then, they used to carve a set of false teeth out of wood for their old people."

Standing at the sink, she shook out the last of the water from the eternal plastic blooms and stuck them one by one into a glass vase.

"Ma, didn't you say that you wanted me to cut your hair?" I asked.

"Hmm. It is beginning to look like a spider's web, isn't it?" She swung her head from side to side, peering at her reflection on the kettle. "Well, if you want to, may as well have it done now." Then she went on about having much to do to prepare a feast for my grandfather. And about burning some more incense. "Besides," she added, "if you don't do it now, who knows when you'll be back again."

My mother sat in the middle of the kitchen, wrapped in a gingham tent pinned around her neck with a clothes peg while I stood behind her and clipped and snipped. She counted on her fingers. "Let's see, your auntie's letter took about a week in coming . . . Anyway, I guess it doesn't matter when we pay obeisance. And I'll have to go shopping down in chinatown. How about Sunday, then? A big dinner on Sunday. Mind you — you remember to come back on Sunday to eat and pay your respects then."

THE WOMAN
DOWNSTAIRS

She runs the corner store, but she doesn't own the establishment. She works long hours, but she doesn't receive any wages. She cooks all the meals, but doesn't have the time to sit down to eat them. She's never been to school, but she's very learned. In fact, she is far better informed on current affairs than this writer, and yet she has never stepped beyond a six-block radius of where she was born. Her name is Helen Hum, but perhaps it's more correct to say that her name is Helen Ho Hum — as in oh well, what can one do really? Long ago, her great-grandfather came to this country with false papers. The immigration officer of the day listed his nationality as "Chink," and further misinterpreted his surname to be Hum. In those days, it was all such a game — tit for tat, or more pointedly, chinese tit for lack of anglo tact.

Decades later, when the Canadian government offered amnesty to those who entered under false pretences, her father thought to regain the true family identity of Ho, more out of patriarchal pride than for the accuracy of federal registries. Amazingly, though, there remained so much resistance to outside jurisdiction from within his rooming house full of doddering old fools that he did a rather halfhearted job of it.

HELEN IS FORTY this year. And Ella M. Carney was fifty-one when she banged out these lines ten years ago. Ten years ago was 1984. Helen has noticed that 1984 was a year that people used to cling to as the future, even if it was full of cold and useless portents. Now it's past. Or old news, as Ella used to say.

Some of us have survived it. In fact, in many ways, thanks to Ella, Helen has quite flourished. But Ella herself got stuck. Hunched over her battered portable, she never got beyond these two paragraphs. Maybe the story she had in mind wasn't interesting enough. Maybe she thought it wouldn't have sold – not even to a local newspaper. (It wouldn't have.) Maybe Ella just thought to hell with it and gave up.

It was started on a plain foolscap, then tucked away among many other pieces of foolscap. Helen was too shocked for words when she came upon it to see herself neatly flattened and so cleanly exposed. For many years she resented the patronizing part about how she had never gone six blocks beyond her father's rooming house.

She did leave once, a long time ago, to go into a hospital. Her tiny body was so flattened and cleanly exposed by a surgeon's knife that she almost died. Of shock – wouldn't you know it? This episode of harrowing trauma happened so early in babyhood that it stayed safely buried beneath just as many foolscap layers of unconscious memory. Until then.

After some time she realized that Ella had been right after all, and she ventured out to visit an orthopedic specialist. She could not suffer one more winter of sleepless early mornings, supported by worn-out foamies, sitting up through bad bouts of pain and conscience by the bay windows, overlooking the lonely, frozen one-way street in the front of her father's hotel, the Union Rooms.

The astonished doctor asked her if she had just recently come to Canada.

"Scoliosis is quite correctable with prompt treatment," claimed the western-trained physician. "I can't understand why you let it get this bad." Warm sympathetic hands touched

Helen's contracted ribs and gently slid along the exposed spoonlike curve in her hip, which sprouted a dangling, toothpick-thin leg. While Helen stood as still as nakedly could be.

Faced against the wall, Helen remembered her mother, and how she used to explain her daughter's shortcomings. "Helen has never been a good sleeper or a good eater." This was all that was offered to the few persons who visited the curtained back room of the corner store beneath the hotel. It seemed to explain young Helen's thin, sickly, misshaped body. In fact, however, this statement better described the mother's eternally sad sense of life, or even attempts at life.

It wasn't so much that Helen, in a heap on the floor, made a hideous sight. It was more like that old saying, "out of sight, out of mind." So her mother tried to keep her unlucky offspring out of her husband's way as much as possible, in order to avoid the denunciations, which eventually wore her out. She never had much of a life. That much Helen could see. As her small daughter, and kept very small, Helen used to look up from her subdued play in that dimmed room to watch her mother's at first wooden, then crumbling, demeanour.

It was no wonder that in later years Helen was so completely taken in by Ella's glossy glamour. It hit her like a full-page fullcolour ad. The big moment of love was like this: 1984. Helen was behind the counter, roosting on her vinyl stool and thumbing through unsold women's magazines from the racks. Not her favourite ones. Those had already been sold. And that nasty little redneck shrimp Ron Talbot walked in. They cast withering looks at each other. Ron knew he was on her shit list, but that had never stopped him before. Helen knew she would have to keep a scrupulous eye on him. Thieving little shit. His white wispy hair with orangey ends, his posh, englishy voice. His phony, oh-so-sublime arrogance. Like he was a skid-row bum for the sport of it. He'd try to lift something. Just watch. Fallen on some rough times had he for a piss-poor excuse.

"You better not try anything, you old shit," Helen immediately warned. "And you're still not paid up." She didn't take her eyes off him as he sniffed the shelves of canned goods. She never forgot the time when from that very same corner he started decking Helen's father with spagetti-and-meatball-loaded missiles. Mr. Ho Hum had ducked behind the refrigerated counter, locked the soldered-down cash register and eventually had to evacuate, running up to the tiny office at the top of the narrow stairs to phone the police. That was a number of years ago, when Ron was younger and more lethal when on a bender, and, true, he did pay the damages and more. Went on the wagon like a Bombay Sapphire, true-blue british army colonel. Pulled together a little class. Even endeared himself to all the crotchety little old chinamen, so much so that he gained a stint in the Union Rooms. Then he fell, in fact, sloshed, right off the wagon.

Ron must have seen Ella slip in and stand off to the side of the fruits and vegetables. He had to show off then, and remarked, all indignant-like, "Wot yew mean, nasty little chinesee mouth? Yew wotch how yew speakee to your sapeeriors."

Drinking steadily, Helen noted, not enough funds to go overboard.

"Oh yeah." Helen could tell right away that he had no money to buy groceries with. "So tell me, Ronnie ol' chap, just what has white superiority gotten you?"

That was when Helen turned her head, just in case his sneaky glances actually meant something, and saw the tallest, most striking woman she had ever laid eyes on, flashing a smile at her. With a mouthful of perfectly strung pearls that dazzled then stunned. Helen was unable to respond. She had to look away, not believing that she could be the recipient of this glittering gaze.

Ron, however, was not one to let such an opportunity go by. He swaggered up to the counter and began his welcome wagon thing. Helen all shy and awkward. He all ribbon and bows, waving his thumb at Helen.

"She may look all twisted up like a corkscrew, but she's tough as nails, ma'am," Ron said to the stranger. "Yew make sure she don't take ya for a ride, if yew know wot I mean."

The woman walked forward on high-heeled suede shoes, right out of *Vogue*, the colour of Santa Fe, matching handmade gloves and felt hat. A sweeping calf-length taupe raincoat, which rustled with each choreographed step. She ignored the shrimp and kept smiling at Helen, who shrank back from the completely foreign smell of expensive perfume. Those eyes were like beacons into Helen's most secret, dark places.

"Cigarettes, if you please, young lady. I'm not familiar with your canadian brands, but I would like low tar." The woman's voice flustered Helen even more. It could not be that she, Helen Ho Hum, was required to make the choice of cigarette brand for this fabulous being. But the woman had already moved on to the Union Confectionary's selection of mints and gums. Then Ron graciously showed her the local newspapers, and she had him pick up the *Sun,* the *Province,* the *Globe and Mail,* the *East* and the *West Ender,* the *Georgia Straight* and the *Buy and Sell* for her.

In this way Helen had plenty of time to gather her wits about her. She expertly bobbed up and down on her bum leg, along the slots of cigarettes until she had eight brands of low-tar cigarettes neatly laid out on the counter and awaiting further instructions.

Two neighbourhood punkers, a boy and a girl, came in, seemingly oblivious to anything. Helen knew what they would buy: a six-pack of Coke and Styrofoam pots of instant ramen noodles. The woman came to pay for her purchases with a thick billfold full of documents, monies and plastic. This she took out of one of the many compartments of a sleek brown leather briefcase.

Ron blurted out what Helen was thinking as well. "Lady, in this neighbourhood, you'd be wise to pack your valuables on your person."

"Thank you," the woman said to Helen alone. "Perhaps I shall see you again." She paused, then added, "I'm going to stay in that hotel across the street for now, but I will need a more permanent place very soon."

Nobody could believe their ears. The Arlington was the worst dive in town. Even their front lobby stank of beer and urine. But, sure enough, they all watched as she tippy-toed her way across the wet street and through a group of jeering street kids huddled in the doorway.

The girl punker spoke up. "Did you notice that she had only one earring on?"

"Aw, a ritzy type like that," replied her boy-toy companion. "It just got lost."

They too stepped out of the store into the wet unknown. Ron slithered away unnoticed, with cans of beans and cranberry in his back pocket. Helen climbed back onto her stool and laboriously waited for the gossipy desk clerk of the Arlington to take his 9:00 p.m. break.

When Ella came to live at the Union Rooms, there were small yet powerful, black-holelike implosions all over the place. Helen put her at the end of the hall, right under her own room and shared her bathroom with her, so as not to start a sino-anglo war over a stray pubic hair. A white woman in their midst. The few old men who were left sputtered and chafed from their stale rooms. And who knew what kind of white woman.

This was exactly it. Helen wouldn't be able to tell you what kind of white woman. Ella did love taking baths and sharing her french wine with Helen, who perched or stood or made herself as comfortable as she could on the toilet seat, or on a crate. She listened for hours on end as Ella reminisced.

"So here I was, at this party, in some man's palace, so impressed that I was there. I floated down those sweeping grand stairs. Everywhere the evening was lit up by huge fierce braziers of fire. No kidding, the place looked like the Acropolis – not now, but then. People on balconies below me. Some kind of architectural wonder cantilevered right over the sea. I, trailing my gold-lamé gown. Oh, the way that dress draped. Rome, you know, when Rome was still hot. I felt like a queen, walked like a queen, head held high. I didn't care that people were watching me and thinking, Aah, how lovely, fresh meat. I mean, whenever they saw an interesting girl alone they never wondered what she did. Vultures. They always thought, who does she . . . bleep-bleep with, you know. I guess it did go to my young and foolish head. For the longest time, I thought I had power. But now I know poor girls like me only fuck with power. . .

"My, my, don't I drink too much, though? But you're a good kid. Pop another bottle of wine, will you, darling, please?

"Tokay d'Alsace. God, what I had to do for a crate of this shit. But what can one do. Aye? Aye?" She giggled and toasted the whole of Vancouver for all its cute little backward ways, her back arched and bosom thrust out in a pose of athletic prowess. Her long arms reached up, lifting a golden wineglass high in the air. "Old dog, new tricks and all that. And Renoir painted with his prick, and all that . . . Aww, I drink too much . . .

"Started at the bottom, I did. Rock, gritty, grimy bottom. Oh boy, those were the good old days. In 1957, I landed a job as a *Time* magazine researcher. And I was finally on my way. New York. Golly, I was excited. Was I ecstatic! You know, I've had all the money and power I've ever wanted . . . or thought I wanted, but you know, I'll never, ever again, have as much fun. My, my, I did take the wrong turn somewhere . . . Not that I was happy in that girly job. Back in those days, all the researchers were smart, usually rich, little girls. We did all the work, and the writers, of the male persuasion, got all the credit. I could have written circles around most of them, but in those days my tits and ass were my tickets to anywhere but there. Always. Anywhere but somewhere . . . Ho hum . . . he, he, he . . . Helen Ho Hum, I drink too much . . . and I surely did miss the boat somewhere . . . "

Finally she slumped back. Passed out. Soapsuds in a saucy ring around her floating breasts. Her wet hair in dark greyish-brown ropes. The cold-water faucet dripped tearlike along her cheeks and neck. Suddenly her face slid off and that was what really frightened Helen.

Years later Helen still thinks about Ella. The other day she was cleaning Ella's room (and she still calls it Ella's room, as a . . . you wouldn't want to call it a memorial . . . to her) and dusting around the new, well, five-year-old word processor at which Helen spends most of her free time now. Before she knew it, there she was again, thumbing through the hundreds of magazines, books and newspapers she had collected in pursuit of Ella's work, and drifting through the thirty-odd scrapbooks that she has filled with Ella's life.

Then it occurred to her that the one thing people usually missed about Ella M. Carney's person was exactly what she wanted them to miss, but on some level, Helen knew right away that she was very ill. Helen just wasn't one to question it at the time. When Helen, like any other little poor girl, found herself a Barbie doll left by the side of the road, she didn't mind that it was used and damaged. In fact, she never knew that it could be anything else.

In all the time that Helen knew her — and in this case, five very intense months was a lot of time – Helen's Barbie had only three outfits. Two of them still hang in the closet – the business-front one, which was what she wore when she swooped in from nowhere, and the sky-blue fleecy sweatshirt and sweatpants that she bought at Army and Navy and thereafter wore day and night.

The most wonderful thing about her was not, obviously, her retinue of apparel (which hangs mute, shrouded in protective black plastic), but the fact that she talked. A lot. And said the most wonderful, whimsical things.

"I was barefoot, you know," said Ella, her very long un-shaved legs poised over the rim of the clawfoot bathtub like a Hanes ad. "Heels fell apart. Well, you can imagine trying to squeeze wolf paws like mine into high-heeled slippers. It just didn't ever work, though many have tried."

That, to Helen, was as true as sunlight in the woods. Ella M. Carney had big bad wolf written all over her. Angular big bones; not just a hungry but a ravaged face; fine white furry down all over her body. And such huge, perfect teeth. Chinese don't like wolf, thought Helen, who couldn't imagine such a strong wolf spirit fitting into anything, or anywhere.

Once, during one of Ella's highs, three-thirty in the morn-ing, she snuck into Helen's room and climbed into bed with her. When Helen woke up, she found Ella nicely relaxed, laid out full length beside her, beaming, and waiting to read her lat-est article to someone. At times like these, when she looked so happy to be alive, Helen would listen to her, no matter what.

"This one is for the *Star Enquirer*. Listen:

PRINCESS MURDERED
CHILDREN LIVE IN TERROR FOR OWN LIVES
Her Serene Highness of ——— was brutally slain, and the grue-some details of her death on that fateful day were skillfully

covered up, according to inside sources. Although well loved the world over, the Princess was deliberately eliminated, simply because she had become a middle-aged embarrassment to her husband, the ruthless Prince Grimy of the Mafiosa cartels that own and control the huge money-making casinos in the Mediterranean.

In an exclusive interview with the Star Enquirer, *close friend and trusted confidante Ella M. Carney, a well-known journalist and ex-wife of French publishing magnate Claude LeBerge, revealed that Her Serene Highness feared for her life because she could not keep up with the rigours of being a Princess on a pedestal, and she knew she had become a burden to her greedy aristocratic relatives, who have murdered unwanted wives and surplus heirs for centuries. This is why her children dare not speak out.*

"The Princess drank heavily," said Carney, "because she was always under a lot of pressure to be a shining example of pure womanhood. How many times have I heard her cry out, 'He's going to kill me! He's going to kill me!' And for what, pray tell? Because the poor, terrified woman had gained a pound or two. Her life was hell. It was as if she was caught in a very bad Hollywood role, and she couldn't get out of it, you know."

"Is this true?" Helen interrupted. After all, she read a lot too, and couldn't be taken in that easily. If Ella used to consort with fairy-tale princesses and the like, then what was she doing on the skids?

"Let's put it this way," rebutted Ella, "if you read, then you know that the princess's life was one long drawn-out newspaper story, not a fairy tale. It makes sense that the people most closely associated with her would be newspaper people like me. She was a perfect snob to me for a long time, because I was too much a contemporary of hers. When I came to know her, I was already managing editor for *Heart's Connoisseur,* and about to be married into *Paris Match*. I was as ambitious, as well-dressed and just as bitchy as she was. And irish to boot. And she was just another redneck american small-town girl, looking for loyal bridesmaids . . . Really, she liked me. We were drinking pals. She was lowlife enough to warn me when I was about to get dumped by my husband. In the end she did me a favour because I had lots of time to get my finances in order and guns in place."

"But why are you doing it this way?" Helen asked.

"Isn't the reason obvious?" she asked, with a twinkle in her eye. "I get turfed out, and she gets knocked off. And I'm going to be next if I don't watch out. There're a lot of us used-up old bags with big mouths out there, and we should all read the *Star Enquirer*, because instead of propaganda we get rumours. And once in a while they may even be rumours of the truth."

Then, of course, came the day that Ella disappeared, wearing her third outfit – new white Gastown leather jacket, pants and boots. Helen had to describe them to the young detective, Moe Hassan, who reluctantly started a file on Ella M. Carney after the required waiting period. The file number was, and continues to be, JF 2649. But the assigned officer has since been changed to Ken Walker – friendlier, more sympathetic than the dark-faced Moe, who has climbed up the ladder, but who once stared at Helen coldly and made her feel very stupid when she tried to explain that Ella M. Carney was just one of the names Ella used.

"She's been married a number of times, you see. How many times? At least seven that she has mentioned to me, sir. I think she said her real name was Cinderella Shoemaker, but maybe she was just making a joke."

How Helen wished that she had enough verve to talk to him as Ella would have talked to him. "Well, you see, Moe. Mr. Hassan. Actually, you know – I have been acquainted with at least two households of Hassan. One so powerful in Iran that it was answerable only to the Shah himself. Many of them reside in Paris now. You wouldn't be related to any of them by any chance, would you?

"No. Of course not. Come to think of it, they were not nice people."

Her hand, large but elegantly bent at the wrist, would have flashed rings and an expensive watch and supported a sharp, almost harsh, chin that would not jerk when she was reminded to get to the point. "Well, as I was about to say, I've led a rich, colourful life. Six – not seven – marriages and countless fucks, just so that I could pile as many aliases as I could between myself and a miserable childhood with retards who would name their kid Cinderella Shoemaker. I think you of all people, Officer Hassan, might understand my loathing for such a disadvantaged start in life."

However, at that critical time, Helen felt cowed by their heartlessness. She dared not offend them, because they were all there was, and besides, she thought, maybe they did have the power to make Ella come back. The police station was only three blocks west, but she wouldn't have ever imagined that she could have ventured so far out on the limb if she were not desperate for any kind of information about Ella.

After nine months and still no trace of her, Officer Ken was kind, new and gung-ho enough to find out that there have in fact been eighteen Cinderella Shoemakers registered at birth within Canada, during the past sixty or so years. One, born fifty-one years ago in Ormsby, Ontario, had to be Ella.

Helen was by then a nervous wreck, jumping at each and every buzz of the shop door when it opened, hoping, praying and fantasizing that it would signal Ella come back. And some days that stupid thing buzzed two hundred and forty-seven times. No kidding. Helen counted. Christmas day is always crazybusy. Christmas day of '85 was freezing, and you had to keep the damned door closed. That day Helen finally had to give up at two hundred and something by midday.

That was the year Helen's father had a stroke, survived it and came home to live in his wheelchair upstairs. And he wouldn't agree to an electrical lift.

"What I want to go down there for? Stupid girl!" he'd bark at her in that mean and nasty way, which has always made her feel creepy and shamed. And it was true that there was no reason for him to come down. If he had gotten so decrepit, then all his old shit friends were very dead. But by then Helen was the boss, and she was thinking of a lift more for herself. And besides, she had already done her worst to him when she went over his head and hired her mother's elder sister's granddaughter and her husband from the village, because although she would continue to take care of his store and hotel, she was not going to knock herself out any more. Besides, she had developed other interests, such as her writing and research. And these were on top of her weekly chiropractic, physiotherapeutic and masseuse appointments. The couple worked out very well, both being ambitious, in love and oh-so-eternally grateful to have gotten out. And they were even fun to have around.

Big Auntie's granddaughter brewed such wonderfully tasty sweet medicinal soups for Helen's dad. He enjoyed her village ways (didn't realize they were wiles), got chicken-'n'-gin souped, and regaled her with sourpuss tales of white people's excesses when he was a young houseboy. She was appropriately horrified at the way a twenty-pound Christmas turkey was done whole here, in the oven. Then everyone in a full-bellied stupor sat around to listen to her exclaim how everything here in the west was better. This was better. That was better. Even her soups tasted better here.

That merry Christmas day, with Uncle Lee Buck's great-granddaughters, May(be) and Sue Lee – thirteen and fifteen years old, both honour students at Windermere Secondary – helping out as well, as they have done on weekends and holidays for the past five years, Helen disconnected the buzzer and dug up the old brass tinkle bell of her youth, all cracked and banged up. She got May(be) to get up on a stepladder to hang it up.

"Auntie, we don't ever even notice the buzzer. We never knew it bothered you."

"Auntie, you can get the kind that you can switch off, you know."

"Auntie, you're getting all christmasy sentimental, you know that."

Yes, all at once, a spiritual calm did settle over her like the black-and-white ending of an old Jimmy Stewart movie. Something resigned. Something resolved. It may have been the end of Ella, but for Helen it was a beginning of sorts. In memorable, yet subtle ways; fairy talelike, with the touch of a magic wand.

$\mathcal{B}$ELLYDANCER:
LEVEL ONE

WHEN I STILL lived among them, my people always told me that I was born into a box. Every time they said that, I always thought the same nasty thing – out of one box and into another. I know all about boxes. I make boxes, I live out of boxes, and I mostly feel safe in them. With them all around me, I'm not a bag lady, I'm a box lady.

My father was murdered two months and two weeks before I was born, you see. My mother was only twenty-one at the time, with a baby still in diapers, and another still wetting the bed. After the murder she tried to keep things together, but five days before I dropped, it came to light that it was my uncle, my father's only brother, her own favourite brother-in-law, who had stabbed her husband to death. She just went to pieces, or, she went "partying" (as my granny euphemistically called her bingeing, until her own death in the snow, some twenty years later). You see, in her grief, and in one moment of weakness, she let this same man find his unscrupulous way between her legs a bit too easily. A pretty mean feat, I would add, with all her little children around and in the way.

Anyway, Mom was so drunk she didn't realize she was cramping real bad. People tell me that at a house party during an early-morning brawl, she suddenly felt an urge to squat, and

I shot out like a bloodied projectile, my little head smacking the linoleum floor like a slap on the bum. People blew that party scene screaming in horror. Apparently I didn't so much as twitch an eyelid; I was so limp and purple they thought I was stillborn. Well, you can imagine me, poor little thing, thoroughly pickled in alcohol, and such an irreverent entry to this world as well!

Then there was that unholy gash where my cute little suckling mouth should have been. Even I have to admit that I would have hurriedly wrapped me in a blanket and put me in a pine box too. I don't know if I would have thrown me on top of the woodpile in the shed, though, but who knows what whoever was the ad-lib undertaker was thinking at the time.

Anyway, that's where my grandma found me two days later, wailing at the top of my little lungs, in the middle of a northern Alberta winter. She figured that big ol' cat named Henry had been glad to have a warm if squirmy blanket in a wooden box to sleep on.

Granny bundled me and my two brothers, Ernest and Edgar, into the cab of her and Granddad's pickup. It was so crowded she had to put me on Granddad's lap as he drove. Together they trundled us over treacherous icy backroads back to their ranch high in the mountains. When Mom sobered up that time, she just followed.

I don't know if this early encounter with a pine box is the reason I make boxes today with such a passion; those guys with white coats would have a heyday with such origins. But what do doctors know of hillbillies, eh? At least I was smart enough not to give them this story to chew on. Yeah, yeah, I've been through their mean sterilizing machine. In one fast hurry too.

So what, I always say. Mom's been dead these past seventeen years. And I figure that if one of my carved boxes is good enough for the Royal Winnipeg Museum of Art – permanent collection, no less – then I say, Hey, eh! Mom, you're OK; I'm OK; every-thing's OK. Granny has always said that Mom was a good woman. I can see that; I saw otherwise too. She tried the best she could, I guess. I can still hear Granny repeating like a treadmill, "Your mom did what she could, I guess." So did I, I guess.

When it came time for me to leave their brown leathery faces, toothy grins and generous hugs, Grandpa stomped his worn cowboy boots, spat into his juice harp and sang:
"Pretty as a filly,
Brighter than a bee.
Send her to the city,
To see what she can be . . . "

Maybe Mom went out there trying to find out what she could be. Myself, I ventured out to see what I could see. I saw plenty, I guess. Enough to know now that I shouldn't have been in such a darn hurry to leave those hills, because I never saw my grandma and grandpa again. They never did know that I be-came famous, that the new owners had to name the restaurant where I once danced Seni's, after me, that Ernie, Edgar and I till keep the ranch, that there's hardtop almost to the gate now.

In my heart, I have always imagined Grandma telling Granddad, because she could read my letters, and he could not, "Seni says she's learning bellydancing, Paw."

"Bellydancin'!" A bear paw harumph. "Bellydancin'? What for, learnin' bellydancin'?" Then I betcha he'd half joke and ca-jole at her for days after that. Time was different for them in those hills.

"Because, Grandma" – and I would have told her because she might have understood a ways, whereas he wouldn't have at all – "when I drape that silk veil over my mouth, I feel like a real queen. The rest of my body suddenly becomes gorgeous, and gorgeous loves to dance. Gorgeous loves to be adorned and adored. I become someone else, Gran. Not Scarface, Gran."

And then of course my grandmother would have said what any grandmother would say: "Now, Seni Biln, you're the prettiest girl we've ever seen. Isn't she, Paw? You'll always be a very special girl to us."

Unless she had had a few too many herself, then another story about my scarred past always got a few snorts.

" 'Member, Paw, that time when Ernest and Edgar had to go and hide out in them Ghostkeeper Hills for three months, after Ern made such a mess out of ol' Mrs. Oddy's boy? Damn, was that ol' shit *upppp*set. Christ, you boys must have been cold up there! 'Member, Paw, even we were melting that brown-coloured ice on the stove for something to drink. Jesus, I fussed and worried and cried for days. With them big ferocious redcoats stomping and tearin' the place up lookin' for you two."

In exasperation my brother Ernie would then have to say, "Man, how many times do I hafta tell you, Gran? Ed and me, we just kept going and thumbed our way clear through to Calgary."

But there was no way that she would believe him. So Ed would have to throw in his two bits: "You know, I still think about that white guy who picked us up. He was kinda decent. Even offered us a job in Phoenix, Arizona, eh? Damn, should have gone and sent our gran a postcard with a cactus on it. Mebbe then she'd believe us, eh?"

A good-natured smile always perking, always warm, always ready. Back then, the only time my twisted mouth relaxed enough to laugh was when I was at home with my grannies, close to the woodstove and listening to them inside stories – this one about the Shoemakers. Tom Shoemaker was nicknamed Mrs. Oddy after a teacher he bit a chunk of flesh off during a scuffle and swallowed in the desperation of the moment. He had been an abused kid who grew into an ornery man who begat Herman, who reduced me to tears when he painted bright red nail polish onto bobby pins, pinned them all over his upper lip and went around the high school imitating my petrified lisp. My big brother Ernie, then too hulkingly shy to string two words together, took the bobby pins off along with his lip with just one swipe. Blood all over the halls. End of Ernest ejacayshun too.

"I make my own costumes, Gran" – I used to talk to her by long-distance telephone – "with beads and sequins, and feathers, and, oh, Granny, you should see, the sheerest of gossamer chiffon."

"Isn't that nice."

"I dye the fabric myself, with a special ancient formula from a real old book. My bellydancing teacher – she got too old to dance any more – says that it's hundreds of years old, Gran. It was the only thing she brought with her. She's a refugee. She says my costumes are real works of art."

"Ain't that wonderful, Paw?" she'd yell off into the background.

"Oh, Granny, I sure wish you could have met her. She was so good to me, picked me up where you left off. I sure do miss you and Grandpaw, Granny."

"You bring her home. Home to visit. What's her name, Seni?"

"Lulu, Gran. But she's long gone too."

My voice to the past fades as I watch the idea of a home to visit swirl down the drain of a sleek hotel bathtub. When I look into the bathroom mirror, I'm surprised to see how much of the misty reflection is still my small face pressed up against the frosty windowpane of their snug log house. It's almost flawless now, but that's something else my grannies never saw.

Two plastic surgeries later, one thin vague line, shaped like an upside-down check mark, remains. They were done by a miracle worker in San Francisco named Dr. Hamazaki. He left my – he called them "exotic" – lips with a heart-shaped courtesan pout, exactly as he drew on his one-of-a-kind colour-graphics computer screen to impress me. Before, after. Watch again. Before, after.

I was greatly impressed, because he was truly an artist. And with an income seven digits long, he had reached sainthood, I'm sure. Furthermore, as his receptionist piously pointed out, I should have been more grovelling grateful, "Because Dr. Hamazaki doesn't usually do show people any more. He's busy enough." By then the filipina actresses and caribbean beauties he had picked up in the early part of his career had all married rich tyrants and were desperately trying on one mask after another to keep up appearances. Apparently there was a more altruistic part to his career; he does slash-and-burn patients for free if he gets written up as a human-interest story in a major magazine. Of course the receptionist didn't use those exact words. I did. I just think it's a slash-and-burn world.

Oh, I was dreadfully grateful for his charity. Of course I was. I remember how I first came to him with a quivering handshake, malnourished, days on a Greyhound, still underaged then – clutching a pitiful bundle of the same twenty-dollar bills that had been stuffed down my sequined bra by countless mauling hands. I didn't even have enough. But to him I was another dirtied brown baby like those from the war-torn places he used to touch down in, with his heroics and golden touch, with his international team of god doctors flying . . . flying. He took pity on me.

Aah, maybe bellydancers get too canny to think of a good enough reason to leave home. I just hate the fragmented being from another time and place that I become when I travel, so I don't any more, except in my head. Yet here I am. I come out of the bathroom and gaze at the four-star-hotel suite. There is a basket of fruit and champagne with a card I cannot bring myself to read. A massage table is already set up. I have a few minutes before my masseuse comes back, so I don't bother getting dressed. I climb naked onto the white sheets and immediately fall asleep.

I awake to the sound of Susie Wong's key in the lock, to the vertigo one feels when being dragged around and about unconsciousness.

Susie looks just as frazzled as I feel, but she hauls up the heavily laden ritual kit and picks out the lemon-grass toner first, exactly as she does before every live performance. And I don't mean only the ones up on stage. She's been with me for six solid years. I'm so grateful that she has come on this expedition that I would have gladly grovelled, except she won't hear of it.

"You'll pay for it." Susie derided my feelings the way mothers do to harden daughters who have to go out there and expose themselves. I have paid for a first-class flight for her, but I know she has endured a ten-hour standby and pocketed the difference – her excuse being homely, married to a bum, with three "hongry kids." I don't care. Every slave needs a slave, I always say. The important thing is that she knows every inch of me. She does her unadorned work of slapping me around, rubbing on the scent of crushed cloves and saffron, helping me slip into fifteen pounds of jingle-jangle. She gets me into the mood.

"What's it going to be today?" She stands there, staring holes through me, already sensing my anxiety. I am quivering with anticipation. At a time like this, I feel I need pain to block the shame. And the rougher, the more familiar. "Deluxe. Super Special or a Real Lulu?"

I pretend I don't need it. Yet I roll over on my back and expose myself completely.

"I don't care," I say. "As long as you do tits and ass and do it hard."

"I don't do cunts," she mocks as she starts. Light insinuations at first, but I know how deep and profound she can get. And I am dying for it and dreading it at the same time.

"I figure a smart lady like you can get that done proper," she adds.

Don't I always swear this is going to be the very last time that I sabotage myself. Scarcely forty hours ago, Susie patiently held the flashlight as I arranged my packed cedar boxes and layers of foam on the floor of my Chrysler van and commented dryly, "You won't fly. You can't decide. You never gonna make it in time."

"Never you mind." I was all wound up, because I knew she was right: I had designed it so that I would make it only at the expense of sleep or, worse, injury to the sacred cow of my body.

"You just make sure you show up." My parting words to her were brusque to protect my fear, then I averted my face from her thin beam of light. As I swung away from the curb, my terrified headlights swept past Susie, her hands lingering on the door handle of her rusty Nissan. And I had to carry the crisis of confidence I created for myself, snivelling, for another hundred miles, perspiring the sour smell of public-phobic stress the rest of the way. Having to face strangers alone is a recurring nightmare of mine, I recoiling at the way they recoil from my nigger-bitch skin, thin scornful nostrils sniffing out my low creeping herbal scents.

Irrational fear. Masked rage. My van, my locked box. I hid from human contact as much as I could, fasting as I went, brewing tea on a camp stove, listening to taped music. Hermit on the I-5 of life, I purged my body daily of toxins, burning incense, euphoric dreams, portable potty, giddy with hunger for I don't know what. I got lost, the second night frozen; high in the interior mountains, teeth chattering, shampooing my hair on plush towels in the idling van, I climbed out to shower under a hillside waterfall, then fell into a fitful sleep. In my dreams, I played a dancer, all right, but a dancer who couldn't perform for the sad life of her.

"But I have made it, haven't I? Here I am." I grin at Lulu, who is close by.

"And I'm done," Susie decides with a slap on my butt. "You look good. You ready for Al?"

"I don't know." I catch my breath.

"Hey, you're breathing too high in your belly. Lower!" she orders. "Relax, will ya!"

I cringe.

"OK, OK, refocus, then."

"I can't." Before I know it, I am shaking uncontrollably; goose bumps all over my naked arms and torso; her work undone. "Susie, help me, please," I cry. "I was wrong to come. I still can't face this."

Susie moves towards me and gathers me into her arms; I shut my eyes and breathe in the warm scent of her hair; she doesn't let go, and I cling and cling.

"Hey, hey, easy now. Yes, you can. Breathe. Look inside. Tell me – what do you see?"

I tell her that I see escape like this: I am going back to see the women at the trailer park. They are my family in the desert. I am cruising down the highway, blinded by sun, hot dry air blasting against my face, dragging through my hair, sucking up every salty grain of moisture. I am sipping lemonade sweetened with maple syrup and heated with cayenne pepper. My little peepot right beside me. On my own again, I am wonderful. I tell her I can dance among friends. I can't dance with the enemy. The donning of veils is too flimsy a cover.

"Honey, go for it, then." She makes it sound so simple.

I dial boss Al on the hotel phone. I sing out, "Al. Seni here.

I can't stay. I gotta head into the desert tonight. Be a sport and cancel my engagements, will ya?" I hang up because I figure he wouldn't care. Small time, I tell myself, small potatoes.

Minutes later, there is knocking at the door as Susie and I are hopping around like mad, stealing hotel towels, giddy with relief.

"Don't forget the fruit basket," I tell her. "The girls at the trailer park will love – "

By the time she opens the door, I am ready to outperform. I make as if I am wallowing in pleasure in the desert heat out on a nineteenth-floor balcony, still as naked and as untamed as the day I was born. Entertained that I am lit up, fluorescent, flashing, wired to my ultra-neon surroundings; always the rasping din of trafficking and the twitching of electricity.

A gross, exhausted man, heaving about on painfully stout legs, steps out into the evening sky and glances not at me but at the last pink glow on a faraway horizon. Leaning against the railings, he asks very patiently, very softly, "What's going on, Seni?"

I haven't seen Al in eight, maybe ten, years. And I am truly dismayed by this miserable version of his former self. I thought I had it bad. This was the wizard who made me famous? Who pushed and bullied and shoved me further than I ever wanted to go. I want to blurt out loud, Never mind me, what the hell happened to you?

Twenty years ago, Al was a hotshot, dynamite – he liked to call himself compere for the lesser-known club acts in Las Vegas. Then, he was full of expressive energy, had an ambitious smile and loved the fun and games of being big daddy – a chunky, jolly kind of daddy-o. He and his lover, Mike, scoffing at Lulu's wheedling, at her french foreign legion accents and theatrical gestures, until that ludicrous moment when she drew the satin veil off me like a magic show. Then their faces fell, awed by my enticing innocence. After my dance, Al gathered me to his thick chest like the scared stiff cardboard doll I was and spoke the traditional line, "Come to Papa."

Today, when he doesn't turn to face me or whatever he has lost, I know: Al got squashed. So who the hell didn't? I rise from the chaise longue, hold out my arms and wait for his eyes to return from their embarrassed retreat. When they finally do, glancing somewhere near my lips, then stumbling down my breasts and along my outstretched arms, he allows himself to come into my embrace. We press against each other, my lightness against his heaviness. My exposure, his balls in chains. I can feel his pudgy hands slide over the silky freedom of my skin.

"Come to Mama!" I whisper into his fleshy ear and feel him tense.

There's either vanity or void. That's something I quietly contemplate all the time. Myself, I prefer void. Less cramped. But I suspect Al is into the vanity of power. Tsk, tsk, Al, what a surefire way to fall short of the big times. I used to hate Al's guts, feared him with a livid passion. He'd crack his big ol' whip, and I'd be made to dance. But isn't that just about the most tired worn-out old war story in this whole wide world?

Vanity or void? At first glance one can just as easily jumble us up, because I'm the one floundering about in vain. I mean, look at me. As hard as I try, I still haven't lost one ounce of my hatred of what he represents to me. All needles and pinpricks around him. And what for? Look at him! At first glance, some wheezy old fart about to go belly up at any moment. Vanity or void, eh? Pitiful either way?

That's why I've learned to stay cocooned in the emptiness of those boxes I carve so passionately. These many winters long, in my warm little cabin, after the dishes, after the snowfall, after the watering, hay and feed, I'd shave and scallop, scoop and tunnel through sweet scented blond wood to my heart's delight. You'd think that I was god carving out a whole new world or something, because by the time I looked up, it'd be springtime, and the river thawing out.

Cedar, walnut, pine, oak, cherry boxes, all with gorgeous wood grain. Hand built, bent and fitted by my brothers. I made them swarm with thick twisting snakes – one pert woman at an art opening referred to them as cosmic serpents, looked at me with amazement, and there I was, trying to hold my wineglass just right.

As a final touch I'd put a japanese paperfold doll inside. One time a series of ten boxes came out of me. I birthed them like children. Then I sold them all. Couldn't keep them anyway, a bag lady like me. They all toddled off rather quickly, though. Hear one got married to a rich art dealer in New York. Vanity or void? I always end up asking myself that.

So here I am, dressed at least, and squealing at Al as he takes me into his office; it is full of flowers, which shocks me because he said they were mine. Eek! Eeek! I hear me, like a plastic squeak toy. Childlike because the older I get, the less I want to know, and being a child is as good a way as any to hold the whole goddamn world in check, if I want. But then I realize.

Al reminds me, "Your dance is still very important to some people. Surely you haven't forgotten them."

But I recall only the years and years of dancing, or was it squirming, in front of guys who couldn't tell the difference. Suddenly I want to change the subject. I say, "I'm threatening to walk out on you, and you're plying me with flowers. Who the hell gets flowers any more?"

"I don't know. They came from all over. Nobody has faithfuls like you do, Sen. A bunch of them have been raising hell at the front desk all week." He watches me the way I feel – an edgy, hungry hummingbird hovering over each bloom, plucking out sappy well-wishes. "A lot of them are little old women pushing little old men around – in wheelchairs, I mean."

"Lulu's refugee crowd," I muse. "At least I'm not the only haunt from the past. They want to see Lulu alive, not me."

"They want to see Lulu's art alive and well." He's still trying to hold Lulu over my head.

"Al," I say, "let's leave her in peace. You and I both know extinct when we see it."

"Maybe they want to see a little faith in Lulu's girl. You know Lulu was the best, but she used to tell people that the way you dance couldn't have been taught. She said it was a spiritual gift – "

"It's true, then," I interrupt, "those rumours of you retiring?"

"Yeah, so?"

"Yeah, well, I can tell." My punch line timed to perfection. I don't want to stick around to hear some fat white guy tell me that dark goddesses are in again, and I should trust what he says because he makes all the rules anyway.

"Listen, Al," I finally say, "I'm sorry. No hard feelings, OK? I don't dance cabaret any more. You've gotten together the best collection of dancers I've ever seen. You've really outdone yourself. Lulu'd've been proud. But nobody's going to miss an over-aged bellydancer – " Oops, I think, slightly overdone; I didn't mean to overdo it, but I did, and do again, " – except other over-aged bellydancers, I guess." Damn, Al does that to me. I look at him.

There's Al gloating for all he weighs now. He's having fun. He doesn't have to say it; he's a sensitive guy, so his slitty eyes say it: Aww, Seni, here I thought you'd have transcended such small peevish things. Al and I go back a long way along a rocky road of you hurt me, so I hold out on you. Old friends, so to speak.

"I'm disappointed to hear that. I didn't think you were the type to hold a grudge or to pull a prima-donna pout on me. You used to be a hell of an artist. Don't forget to take your flowers, though. I was just saving them for you onstage. It would have been a nice touch, don't you think?"

Oh, don't I just grit my teeth. I hate having my nose rubbed in what I want so badly to forget, because it's over, dead and gone. Lulu, Al and I used to swim in the beauty we so lovingly created for each other. Together we wove a fabulous dream, but we blinked our eyes, didn't we, Al? The mirage dried up. And since then I've slapped and rubbed and pinched, but this cultural wasteland is not going to go away. Dying roses, gushy sentimental gestures won't do it. Sorry if Papa can't stage meaning and romance back into our crumbling lives, no matter how much he wants it back. No matter how much I pretend that I don't want it back.

"I don't suppose we got you to sign a contract – " Al tries a hard poke of reality, after he couldn't say it with flowers.

I laugh and laugh at him, but my laughter is a hard eggshell; inside a wet, ugly duckling still cringes from him. Too many years of him paddling my butt. I want to tell him off so much. OK, Al, it turns out there are lots of hard feelings 'kay! No matter what, you'll always be the white-slave trader, and I'll always be the black pair of tits. That doesn't give either of us much credibility. But I don't say any of that. Neither do I say, So sue me! Just you try suing an indian, see how far you get. Al, you son of a turtle, you paid me to show up. I showed up, and now my mind flits off. When I get to some deserted canyon somewhere, tell you what, I'll fete fire and dance my little heart out in honour of your retirement. Al, sweetheart, you've always gotten away cheap.

I am silent. Maybe the trouble is that I don't ever say enough to Al. Maybe that's been our one saving grace.

"You going by the trailer park?" he asks.

"You betcha." I gather up my overcompensated pride, make gestures to leave.

"No one's there, Seni. The girls are all on their way here to see you." He takes me by my arm and puts me out of his office. Before he closes his door in my duped face, he says, "I understand that you need to rest tonight, sweetie. That's OK. We can do without. But tomorrow I need you for some crowd teasers. I still have to fill up the amphitheatre. Seni, darling, if you want for anything at all, feel free to talk to my girl."

I am truly touched. Al's one smart bitch. I guess he knows it. So here I am. I know I am loved. And I am walking along the edge of the crowded casino. I am shimmering satin, flowing show, tripping on tiptoes. I get lots of attention. And I give a lot back. Crowd teasers, said the man. In this way, I'm a professional right down to my choice of lady luck emerald green, wild desert blooms clipped onto dense black wavy hair. I move through the crowds of tourists milling around, smoking, looking. Slot-machine cycles are up, yeasty housewives swarming. They're looking for something too; their laundered househusbands in cheap, crisp hawaiian shirts look at me. It's nice to be appreciated, and Al sure has taken a lot of trouble to get me here and to keep me here.

Oh, look, I spy cowboys. Ohh. And they're cowboys and indians too. Love those cowboy and indian colours. These ones tall and slim and dark and cowboy chic. I see a silver-and-turquoise bracelet clipped over an embroidered cuff, bolo ties, the spit and pearly polish of skin-tight black boa boots, and I can't help smiling my approval. These ones traditional; they wear their wealth unabashedly. They pause in frank surprise, then flash their teeth in delight. And they are absolutely delightful. Sky-blue teardrops weigh down an old-fashioned, blackbrimmed reservation hat. They all tip theirs. Duster coats sweep the floor. Life is a feast, and I pass through, my tongue moist, ready to taste.

$\mathcal{B}$ELLYDANCER:
LEVEL TWO

SO I SEE HER. Lulu's girl. Seni's sidled up to some skins. My love in shadows – I watch her weave her magic. She is telling them about her show. They begin to flow with her movements. They catch every silken word, watch her hypnotic mouth give form and take it away. She sways, pressing towards them; they hover in. Tall mountains, hard rim rock, tawny faces lit up by the rippling yellow streaks of light after a cloudburst. They watch her go, as lovely as the final days of summer. Hands grasping discount coupons.

"We'll be there," they call out after her.

Yeah, they'll be there. And Lulu's dancing girl keeps prowling. She knows where to find them. Get too close to the big gaming tables and nobody will even bat an eye at a bellydancer, so intent are they on all or nothing. She spreads out a little. The bar scene, the clones of leather boys . . . and girls, indian country, artists, cowboys, druggies, the hollywood talent scouts, the shop girls. The hotel lobby scene, musicians, wannabes with money, the gonnabes with never enough. Of course, what Al the puppeteer meant by crowd teasers is the box office crowd, tourists, big pasty kids with filthy minds and smeared mouths. Lulu's girl in full peep-show regalia. Give me a hit, they gasp. And she whacks them but good.

Of course what Al says is not the same as what Seni does. I follow her, knowing it won't be long before she makes her connection. Uh-oh, there she goes. And, shoot, it's that greaseball punk what's-his-name!

"What's your name again?" asks Seni, even though it's a lethal question in our line of business. But he spotted her; she didn't have time to get away.

"Jimmy Polk Knox," he replies, his face going through the many shrewd expressions of hollywood talent-scout interest. Betcha she's surprised that he's still alive. No, she's not. He's white.

"You're Al's girl, aren't you? Semi? Zany? Aah, yes, I remember now . . . seamy, steamy, hot . . . Seni. Am I right?"

Seni grins.

"Right, in for Al's big international dance show, I betcha."

Seni cocks her head, shifts all her weight onto one foot, tightens her crotch and slides one leg against the other.

"The best ball-bustiest l'il missy bellydancer in the whole damn country, as I recall, Seni. All right."

Seni raises an eyebrow and says distractedly, "Jimmy Polk? Have y'all seen Andrades around?"

"Naw, heard he went back to the ghetto. Whaddya want with that troublemaker? Him and his oily drum thumpers. Good riddance!"

Andy back to L.A.? Who was Al using for her backup, then? She had just assumed that it was going to be Andy. They're naturals together; he follows her every twist and turn as if they shared the same body, never forgets a routine and plays everything from cello to clay flutes. Oh well, he may be coming in yet.

"Where do Jah Thoughts hang out, Mr. Jimmy?"

"Jah Thoughts," he hoots. "In the cracks, of course! Haw, haw, haw!"

Jah Thoughts was a dance troupe of odd sorts. If Seni finds
them, she will have found the trailer-park girls. They once
formed a large coalition of street performers who came together
because someone found a deserted warehouse with a sprung
maple floor, and lasted until the place got torched for insurance
money. Jimmy Polk's scoff is a good sign that maybe dark
women are still thriving in spite of the odds. By now he's
putting two and two together.

"You better watch out. You just might get flushed away, l'il
missy." Jimmy Polk's the can't-help-hisself type. Seni moves
away; I stay with her.

"Aah! Those dykes don't call themselves Jah Thoughts any
more," he calls out after her, surprised that she's not begging for
blow. "I kinda liked Gorilla Girls myself, but they're all growed
up, so they call themselves L.A. Bush Women now. Try Los
Antros, alias hole to piss in."

I just love to watch Seni move. She enters the bar rather
timidly, but when she sees that her kind of people are here
and in great numbers, she struts in spectacular style. Before
long, her hips are a-swingin' and a-mowin' down a wide path
through tables crowded with old friends. The Mercy Mees,
backup singers, and flaming queens falling down on their knees
in abject goddess worship. She in skin tights, strap sandals and
a blinding white handkerchief shirt made of south asian cotton
so fine and supple it moves like liquid. A choking clasp of ama-
zonite surrounded by sweatlike beads of glass and carnelian on
braids of indian cured leather around her swirling waist.
She plays with them awhile – a dancer's entry to a tough
audience of dancers, bowing, gesturing, grovelling grateful.

Finally Seni spots a big round table at the back. The women
at the table see her and go berserk. As noisy as the bar is, she
hears the trailer-park women squealing like squeak toys, wolf
whistles, hoochie-koochie. There are Rosalie and Irma pretend-

ing to be forty, everybody teeny-bopping incredibly fluorescent headfuls of hair, bouncing their tight pink-flesh-filled bodices. Wild minxes, it must have been a long time since they've been let out of their cages, I think, while Seni heads straight into their arms.

Bellydancers don't tolerate being alone. It's the nature of our beasts. As exhausted as Seni was, I knew she would not rest until she had found the trailer-park girls; they are family, and probably the real reason she ventured out this far. She hasn't seen them for eight years, not since Lulu's funeral.

Later, in Seni's hotel room, they are all still giggling and pinching themselves. To the barnyard sound of ten females trying to shower, pee and shave their armpits in the same bathroom, Seni loses consciousness so fast that they tell her afterward that she almost twitched off the king-sized bed. The next morning, she wakes gently, her ears filled with soft droning snores, a short nose pressed against massive perfumed cleavage.

"Rosalie?" she asks.

"Yeah, hon?" Her age-old stage name was Rosalie Thumper. Now post-Lulu, she's one of the grand dames.

"Didn't Al get y'all a room?"

"Sure he did," she replies. "But it's way off the map, and it's a real dump." A throaty voice culminates in a coyote yawn. Californah Penny, the blond pinup girl, stirs. Seni lifts her head and spies Susie Wong, her batwoman, fully clothed, way off by herself. Ever faithful, she had spent the night on a cramped couch in the corner, clutching a cushion, close by their packed luggage, just in wooden case. The others are still snoring.

"But there are more of us," adds Rosalie. "You haven't met the newest girl. We call her Starface. Isn't that terrible? Her real name is . . . shoot, what's Star's real name again?"

"Joan," says another woman, waking.

"Right. And then, you know, Carmella's mom wanted to

come. Then her sister had to come too. Next thing you know, the whole tribe's here. Some of the guys are sleeping out in the cars. Joe's got a room next door. Motel, you know. Anyway, it's sure not like this place. Al treats you good, Seni. Not that we're complaining, you understand. When he sent us those fancy invites to his show and retirement party, Irm and I thought we done died and gone to heaven."

"You still got Joe buzzing around you, Rosalie!" Seni, happy to be home again, snuggles closer to her. Rosalie's long arms tighten around her.

"Why not? He's my very own cousin. We all getting on. We more like housewives. Same ol' fellas over and over again. Only they stay longer, brawl less, sleep more and pay more. Shoot, girl, some nights I still haul in more than Marilyn Monroe here."

She nudges Penny, who is quick to respond, "You dreamin', Mama!"

"Seni, you should see my flower garden now. Is it ever bewwtiful . . . " Rosalie starts to say, but that is too much old-lady talk, and Gwendolyn asks to see Seni's jewellery. Cocoa says, "Yeah," and the whole place jumps into action. Boxes spring open like jumping jacks. Girls ooh and aah over treasure. Susie gives up protective custody after some pushing and shoving. Seni mentions she's hungry; Rosalie is on the phone: "What do you mean, breakfast for ten is the only room service this room gets? Tell Al he's a cheapskate!" But she is pleased — dimple pleased.

It is Californah Penny who mentions me first. Bitch! A thousand paddle whacks across her swollen ass wouldn't be enough. She'd just squirm and shudder in sweaty delight. We've done it to her before. There ain't nuthing that bitch won't pull. It takes a tough gang boss like Rosalie Thumper and Co. to keep her halfway in line. They are talking about Starface, saying she got her name because she was beaten so bad that she still sees stars all over the place. Penny wrapping thin pale gold over her arms and around her neck. She has loved those same roman coinlike pieces for ages. They match her fine pastel hair, and make her look hollywood paganlike. Always hard to decide if she's being malicious or just plain stupid on purpose. Anyway, she pipes in, and the room freezes, "Star always reminds me of Rita."

I was Lulu's girl too. Out of desperation, I brought Seni to Lulu. Way back then, when she was scared and sick, with a face like a mashed-up doll's. Funny how I still see that soft, pliable, tear-streaked look on Seni's face today. Even if it is all grown up, not about to be destroyed. This doesn't mean it's not gullible, though. Seni startles at the mention of me.

"Is Rita here too?" She turns to Rosalie, about to scuttle back into her arms. The rest of the girls, a messy chain reaction of surprise, of embarrassment, of evasiveness, mop up the spill as fast as they can. I see genuine slapstick. Gwendolyn and Cocoa make threatening moves on Penny. They shove her, and she squawks at the affront. Rosalie bellows, "Not with that jewellery on, you don't."

Penny takes the opportunity to swing at Gwendolyn, who is, of course, expecting it. Rosalie's voice goes berserk. "I said take that jewellery off. Another move, Penny, and you're out. I mean it." The two black women catch Penny's arms, force her to her knees and hold her down. Rosalie clucks indelicately, as she delicately peels Seni's hard-won medals off her.

"Honestly. Can't take you wildcats out. Look at this place, a classy joint and torn to shreds in no time. Jeez, at home, I'da thrown y'all out into the streets to make a dusty spectacle of yourselves. But what can I do here? Throw you out of a twenty-storey window. But I won't have you embarrassing Irma and me either. No way! We've got our sense of decorum, even if you hillbillies don't. Californah, if you don't behave, I'm just goin' to have Joe stick you with your medicine and take you back home. I mean it. I ain't goin' t'be takin' this shit for long. Now clean up. I mean it."

Seni whimpers, "Rosalie..."

Rosie truly looks concerned. "Well, sweetie, we really haven't seen, ah, Rita for quite a few years, so how would we know?" She bites her lip and does the best she can, and some of the girls can't help but snicker a bit.

What do you know, you old bag! Nuthin'! Like what do you do to get a wild kitten to come to you? I guess you know that much, since it ain't much to know to begin with. You feed it. That's what I did. Back in Vancouver, I took Seni to Frankie Chin's café and bought her a cheap dinner of oolichans with boiled potatoes for a buck fifty. Even late at night a country girl needs her boiled potatoes, I always say. Sat across from her and watched the embarrassment about her love-bruised mouth, her big brown eyes slanted, her complexion ashen with grey edges, her fur wet and matted. Scared and suspicious of most everything. And oh, so vulnerable, she didn't breathe, she panted.

Seni needed me, and I wanted her. I came to protect her after she'd been beaten and penetrated. That night it was particularly brutal and senseless. At seventeen Seni hadn't figured out that none of it has to make sense. When she came to and uncrossed her eyes, she saw me standing in the dark by the window five tenement floors up, preparing to bar her nightmarish flight out. She didn't have to move her bleeding mouth to form words for me. I did all the talking. I told her that I was just like one of those girls back home – the bestest friends she ever had – then left without a thought, to follow a charming drunk into the city. And she never even missed me until she got sad and lonely, did she?

Then, night after night, after her shows, I'd come along and

say to her, "Come on, Seni. Let's go get some Coke and eats."
She'd trip along the dark wet streets, mostly happy again, few
worries except she was scared of one of those drippy-nosed
boyfriends of hers. This one was weird, she said, and she was
supposed to stay put until he came back, that is, if and when he
came back for his bitch. But I knew his schedule by then. Sen's
such a baby, she'll never know just how disposable she was
then. Some of those assholes don't even bother to wipe. But a
couple of hits always got them out of the way, and I'd come
downtown to watch her move.

In those days Seni didn't dance. She jutted out her luscious
butt at men who sneered while they paid. She shimmied
shamelessly. She split wide open and wanted to die in ecstasy.
In those days she stripped herself down to nothing, pounded
herself out on johns. There was nothing slow and easy about
the way Seni tormented herself. This, of course, made me desperate for her.

I'd get her stuff just to get her in the mood to listen to me. If
I came straight out and told her that I loved her, she'd sneer
and twist my meaning around until it sounded more like I
hated her. No, I waited until she thought she was alone. And
I'd let her gain a bit of distance, but then I'd crawl into her
flophouse bed beside her and hold on tight. For a few seconds
at a time our eyes would meet and blaze skyward, into the wild
blue yonder. It wasn't much, but it was enough; I got her used
to staring at me, not at the shit around us. We'd gaze wide-
eyed, held in amazement at the absolute sexual communion
between us.

Of course she used to fight me too. She'd get all confused
and run away. I'd follow the scraping of her stilettos along
frozen pavement, keep track of the poking needles in between
her sodden toes. Pleading with her. Wanting her to come to the
chinaman's with me. Trying to hold her back, as she giggled

and slid down that black hole. Then she really OD'd on some bad shit. And there she was, beside a stinking public toilet, below street level, flat as a pancake, and I thought she was going to die. That was the first time I dared bring her home to the tiny studio in the West End that I shared with Lulu. More correctly, Lulu paid the bills and I paid her back however she wanted.

That night three Yellow cabbies told me to fuck off when they saw Seni. Finally a Black cab driven by an east indian guy took her. He kept staring at Seni and finally mentioned, "She ain't no squaw. She's one of us." Under the circumstances, who the hell cared? All I knew was that I'd have her in my bed finally. Safe and warm and all mine by the time Lulu woke me up with a start.

"Babe, babe." Lulu's voice stroked my throat. "What have you found? Aah, the little stripper who's been inflaming you!" She looked again, appreciatively. "Ah yes, of course, a little rag doll for my own little dolly, am I right? But what if she dies, my pet? How do we explain such a beautiful corpse in our cosy little nest?"

Lulu was a wizard at survival herself, so she did not begrudge anyone else that amazing ability. Especially tender, slender, dark women who pull back from the easy lure of suicide and sit up shakily to take spoonfuls of canned tomato soup and to swallow the last of their bitter tears before they go on. And now, after twenty years, then some.

Last night, my eyes open, I stared at the ceiling of Seni's hotel room where she slept, safe in her tribe, but I, the other, had another one of those waking dreams about Lulu. She and I were in a garden built over sky and sea by artisans with other-worldly skills; the walkways lapped by gentle waves. Hewn out of the most beautiful of trees, spiral pillars of vinelike datura gave cooling shade. The bird on the horizon spread her wings of yellow brilliance, erupted into flight. Lulu and I stood in the turbulence, the wind whipping our hair and veils into the throes of ecstasy. I wanted to watch the sunset but, no, Lulu wanted to show me the leather-bound hawk on her leather-bound arm. I stared at the leather and thought it thick and oppressive, a crafted, masklike shroud over the hawk's eyes. Her pointy feathers bristled with horrible rage, her talons tethered. When next I saw the hawk, her wings, pinioned or broken, flapped against the dust on the ground. Every morning, the dark side of me wakes up to this toxic toilet bowl of a world, my unresolved junkie heap of a body and soul, and I know, of course I know, what I still cannot get free of.

Over breakfast Rosalie examines Seni, looks for traces of me. She breaks into her little pep talk.

"Seni, you're OK. You're fine, aren't you? Heck, girl, you certainly look squeaky clean. A little stage fright maybe, but hey, that's what we're here for. No need to hide from us, honey. We all Lulu's girls. We all refugees here. And don't think that I don't remember how hard it was for you . . . to struggle free of Rita, I mean . . . "

Seni pops her head up. Suddenly she says, "But, Rosalie, you don't understand. I came back for that other side of me. Now that I'm better, I want to reconnect."

So I heard her, I heard her the same as everybody else. She said she had come back for me.

I can't say exactly when Seni started to get ahead of me; I just remember how Lulu took the shrunken pea that was Seni and poked it back into the warmth and wetness of her own passions. And we both watched each fine curlicued tendril unfold, held the total beauty of a woman rebirthing herself in our arms and nibbled of the fruit.

Seni could dance. She did what she was told and made a good, then very good, living for Lulu. And me, I guess. I too danced well, but Seni danced to a spiritual calling. She twirled around and scattered unbearable pleasure and pathos. She breathed life into people's rebellion – sometimes soft pliant magic, oftentimes pounding purges, whereas I struggled endlessly against ladened thighs. Each leg lift clumsy, my hand gestures limp, artificial, incomplete. I felt naked, angry, wanted to squash those buglike eyes into a pulpy bloodied mess under the souls of my feet, my pretty silver anklets all the purer in the gore.

"Think! Are you dancing for them, or yourself?" Lulu would nag me, not at first, but later, after Seni had revealed herself. Then even Lulu, with her long-standing greco-roman nose for money, began to recall the forgotten secret of our dance.

"You see, you're not the one who is naked. They are," she drummed into me, meaning the ones who slobbered over the cute blue-checkered tablecloths and rubbed themselves against their wine bottles, and who squirted into their wives' brighter than white laundry. And the wife ones, happy that they had been taken out by their lovers (*sic*), later found themselves politely squirming in their worn-out girdles, an embarrassed smile beneath their crinkled noses, which were being made to rub against the moist of my breasts encased in coincups size B. Jingling, dangling, jiggling, wiggling. I'm not the one who is naked, I ululate in triumph. They are.

One old broad stood up, wound up her left hook and slugged her old man's paunch. Just like that. Ommph. Most of them, however, made me their target. Hot tea-splattered stains still on my shoulders. I ducked just in time for another to miss my face. Murderous rage, these women forced to drown their daughters, their beauty, their feelings in a roiling pool of toxic hate. My dance, the dance of creation, used to be for them, for women about to give birth.

Yet Lulu's girls do survive and thrive against all odds. They go on and on forever with their erotic powers. Seni was Lulu's shining star in all respects. At the height of Seni's career, we toured Europe.

Lulu set about gorging on the opulence of Seni's *danse du ventre,* as the french so charmingly called it, but after so many years of deprivation, she found it too much, and started up with the booze. Lulu once lived a life of privilege, used to dance in Paris with rose petals at her feet before she escaped by the skin of her chattering teeth, with nothing but demons to live by. She seemed to get old and tired, choking on bad memories wherever she sat down, while Seni and I stroked each other, as restless and as endless as sun annihilating sea. On the hillsides in southern France, within the tiers of balconies, terraces, behind wooden slats and heavy drapes, we, unseen, entwined in each other's arms.

Day and night, Seni played as only the young can. To the hilt. And such playmates. Seni enticed a japanese man, not so young, who could not leave her alone. He took her to Africa, where Seni first got the idea of looking for dried-up family roots, or something that I never much understood. And she left Lulu holding the bag in that horribly fashionable Mar Menor resort. Of course Lulu was furious, but quite frankly her hangovers were too hard to take. She drunkenly disowned us as Seni and I rattled and bounced along train tracks through desert and grassland, swamps in Sudan, on our way to Nairobi and its bazaars and curio shops beneath the gleaming white colonial architecture.

The man and his friends showed Seni how to make the most delightful, amusing paperfold dolls. And Seni is so easily amused. The man was in love with her, was curious about how she managed to keep her charming purity, and probably wrote sentimentally about her in his memoirs.

After that, Seni went back many times. To find her family in the desert, she said. Or, as I teased back, to get bogged down in the sands of time, but I was happy to see her excited.

Bric-a-brac. I saw nothing but made-in-Taiwan plastic junk, but Seni saw endless possibilities in everything. In Africa, Seni gathered meaning everywhere and travelled to more and more remote shores of the desert to peer into the richly woven texture. She had a way with sullen natives. The local women stared impassively at her because they knew who she was even if she, as yet, did not.

Finally Lulu gave up on trying to turn Seni into a performing flea, dried off and even graciously joined us. As sagaciously as a street urchin, Lulu came to offer her imperial tongues to allow native women clear passage home. In Nairobi she helped find Seni's family – well-to-do, converted Muslim slumlords and moneylenders whose senior wives gaped at Seni in astonishment.

"A bastard!" they whispered. "At our door? What does this mean?"

Seni wouldn't have gotten so far as their inner garden if Lulu's kind of nose and nosiness wasn't narrow, arrogant and pale. Seni made shy for a change; they made me furious. I made Seni sit up as presumptuous as all get-out, performance smile, sharp eyes slicing through everything.

"Yes," agreed the filmy-starry sarees, the perfect red fingernails, the heavy black kohl eye slits, finally, " . . . they are remembering that one of the Old Man's last wives was having two sons. She was a native girl, and . . . how you say, not a temple dancer, oh yes, and how very, very funny, a bellydancer. But she was no good. She ran away. Her two sons ran away . . . How can it be that they became your father and uncle in Canada?" They smiled, offering Seni local coffee made sickeningly sweet.

So now, how long has it been since Seni ran back up those hills. And since Lulu, after a lifetime of a thousand and one sweet poignancies, gave up the ghost. And I was set adrift. It's just time after all, and time dunes all around me and my love in shadows.

But before I go – just because nothing beats the epic bizarrity of real life anyway – I must tell of another time when Seni was absolutely alone, and she conjured me up out of her relentless pain.

She was alone in the savannah, in stark contrast, and was clinging for dear life to a large Land-Rover parked in a grassland park, waiting for the rainy season, because a local festival was to happen at the coming of the rains. For days and days, she waited until she lost sense of time, endless clouds rolling overhead as she lay on the roof of the vehicle and stared at the perfect serendipity of reality gone topsy-turvy.

It was a time when she was finally able to grieve for herself in this faraway place, wrapped in a grimy sleeping bag, watching tiny silhouettes of people get beaten by windswept dust. At home she wouldn't have been able to see the slow shadowy erosion that was her life. But here it was all so clear. With us, I had the means; a little bag of white powder dangling off the rearview mirror offered us the choice of a clean life or a clear death. One was so easy, and one was so hard, but I couldn't decide which was what, so she stepped in and told me that the decision wasn't even mine.

"Go to sleep," she told me, "while I watch over you." Then, when the snakes came and dropped all over me, she went to work absorbing my demons, one by one, until they started to overwhelm me. She sat over me, her slick bellydancing legs clenched around my sweating torso, as I twisted and writhed, as the demons crawled in through my orifices and ate at my insides. She let me scream long and hard and far into the night while she chanted with her thin little voice, "I love you. Stay with me. I love you. Stay with me."

I was so deep into our nightmare that I would have drowned if she hadn't pressed our mouths together and breathed for me. In this way she kept me alive by cleaving to my limp body, my breasts warmed by hers, my legs gently undulating between hers, as we swam towards the light above us. Finally, towards morning, we broke surface. I was again able to feel her finger strokes on my face, her lips planted on my nipples, hands massaging life back into both of us.

The little bag dangled over her, shuddered in the wind. All along she kept the choice within reach. Then the rains came. So long had been her sweet anticipation of being washed clean by heaven's downpour that she yanked me out into the mud and tore off my clothes. She scrubbed and scrubbed, wanting me to clean up my act. Suddenly, without warning, she tore up the bag and scattered its tragic white magic on the ground. The pelting rain dissolved it.

"You dumb bitch gone crazy," I howled at her with all my shaking, impotent rage, while she, persistent with her dull dragging healing work, with her crone-bent back, painstakingly restored power.

In the same way she gathered small twigs and twisted branches for the night fires that people huddled around to stave off the cold black huge yawning chasm pressing in on them. The locals didn't think she'd last. They tried and tested her and even tried to frighten her off; one unclean, deranged dark woman without a man, with a big jeep, didn't make sense to them. They didn't make sense to me either, but Seni kept her distance, observed protocol, worked like the other women and had nothing to lose. Besides, she let them drive the rented vehicle. In circles.

Until arm in arm Seni and I circled the throngs of stunning young revellers, all teasing and vying for attention, flashing their teeth in the sun. And the whites of their eyes gleamed against the yellow face powder that accentuated their long perfect noses. Embroidered and bedecked with sunflowers, handiwork and trinkets. Masters and jokers in the art of coquetry. And Seni teased and gestured right back with her roundness to their height, with her foreignness to their comeliness. Her erotic dance was an instant hit in this festive gathering of herders of kinship ties.

Here, the local girls chose their yokel boys, had wondrous fun, tenderly made out, and the next year they all came back to show off the gorgeous big babies that they had made. And the elders made traditional speeches and songs at the instant marriages, and remarriages, the baby namings with no strings attached. The mothers and grandmothers laughed and gossiped over the fond memories of their own love liaisons.

I wondered about these queer little festivals, like all goodness, like soft green oases in great heaving harsh deserts, driven into obscurity by our glutted western meat-market version of romantic love.

And life is the moment: the moment that Seni approaches from a great arid, shimmering distance to meld completely with me. Her slim hips swaying, her pliant arms beckoning, her love offered as my own.

Seni, women like you and I are not supposed to live long enough to tell our stories. Always peering beyond my shoulders, always cringing from blows, real and imagined, I had gotten used to seeing death in the night. And that night, I still pulled back again from the dream, from the understanding, from the spirit.

"Oh, Seni, stop being such a cornflake. It's fucking freezing here after dark," I said as I resisted her caresses. In the tent I couldn't sleep, Seni so vulnerable and female and alone. "After all, those people are other. What can you expect from them? Just another bunch of drunk, horny, stoned men. And girl, that always spells trouble. Remember you are never a slut until you say no."

The thin stream of a bamboo flute, pleasantly zhagareet, whining like a child into the long, cold night, but maybe also sorrowing like a mother, but maybe also turning, curdling into fierce whispering of a crone. A forlorn ululating cry. Seni snoring adorably.

The next morning, intense sunlit heat crept in and billowed our tent out like a bright balloon. By the time I came to, Seni had squirmed out from under the covers, spread out, glistening with perspiration. And I saw them long before they happened. You see, glowing off her perfect skin, the very distinct images of orchids, purplish flowers of love, as a tiny budding ovary on her forehead, with spreading red lips over her heart. Thick petalled and blue bearded just below her belly button.

BELLYDANCER:
LEVEL THREE

SO AT THE START of our journey, I mention to Seni that I
.think tattoos must have more pizzazz on dark skin. Her tattoos
look a lot better to me after all these years. She must touch
them up, eh? They kinda glow. I haven't ever seen tattoos look
so . . . fascinating, I guess.

"OK, Seni," I say, "little girl, I concede to your better
bellydancing judgement. Tattoos are kinky, and sexy, and exotic. In fact, I'd be the first to say that the one on your belly
was inspired. The one on your boobs obscenely overdone, but
who would have thought, you dumb broad, you would dis-
figure your own goddamn face? And right after all that plastic
surgery too. Remember?"

Oh, but I remember how upset I was back then. I felt like
suing the pants off her. I did. I really did. Ruined herself for the
big establishments. Cabaret was dying fast, and it was hard
enough to find work for her, even if she was the one and only.
At the time, I still had a two-year lease on her. Japan was in the
works for her, but over there the geeks all want Mom's apple
pie, not cult.

OK, OK, so I was a bit put out, and so help me, lord-god-
money, I did tear her contract to pieces right in front of her,
with my teeth for emphasis.

"You're goddamn fired," I did say to her, stupidly of course, but I didn't think she'd take me seriously. I guess I'm an emotional kind of guy, and I thought we were family. Or friends at least, weren't we? I mean, I used to scream "You're fired" at Lulu too, but she never took it so hard.

"Al," she'd drawl back at me instead, "you are one hell of a punctilious pimp."

I tell Seni that I was disappointed, that's all. Without any warning at all, she disappeared for eight years. I lost her and Lulu both at the same time. "That broke my heart," I say.

Glancing over at Seni, well, I must have said something that hit a soft spot. She is gazing at me as I drive, though I can't really see her eyes behind her shades, and she says, "At least I sent you Christmas cards. You never even did that."

"We don't do Santa here in the desert. Besides, you didn't send them. Your brother Ernie sent them." But I make sure I laugh good-naturedly.

"Yeah, but I told him he could," she says.

Sure, Seni, anything the pretty lunatic wants. But goddamnit, I don't dare say that. Might set off another psychotic snit that'll last another eight years.

But let's let bygones be gone, I always say. After all, I don't want any more white man's burden on my poor old conscience, do I? And it did do my broken heart good to see her at my party. It was a great party. People came up to slap me on the back and said, "Great retirement bash, Al. Only aren't you too young to retire?" Or "Reeally greeat shew, Al Sullivan." You know, dumb stuff like that. Stuff they wouldn't dream of saying to me when I'm sober. But it's true, I am history now. And it was a helluva show.

"Nobody does artists like I do, do they?" I ask.

"Nope," she answers.

"Whaddya mean no?" I have to ask because that reply could

have a double meaning to it, and I am never too sure of what Seni means.

"Yeah, I meant yeah, Al."

Well, I'm a sensitive guy. Seni and I have always had a limited work vocabulary, but the goddamn meanings that could fit in there! But that's how women manipulate, isn't it?

OK, OK I'd be the first to admit that I didn't . . . don't treat women so good. Yet, you know, I've always liked women. I mean, I really love them. Their tapered hands, their bangles and danglies, that extra layer of fat. I mean, I don't want to wax sentimental or anything like that. Me of all people. I have always had to be tough. On myself and those who work with me. But let's face it, women, all women, will manipulate the hell out of you.

"Hey, listen," I say, "I am not one of those guys who'll beat the shit out of anything female. I know women are put into that position. Hell, we're all put into shitty positions by this here system. I just want to be friends. Go ahead, if you were me, try going up to my secretary and saying something nice like I just want to be your friend, and have opportunities for some intimate little exchanges, like being caught in a shabby little toilet somewhere, so that I can watch you repair your crumbling face, while we discuss Dora's AA potluck last night so that I might have a place to refugee to when I'm old and . . . retired, say? I bet she flicks you off like dandruff. Heck, I have always found that that's how they operate. Not in words, mind you; they look smug, as if they know something. Heck, maybe they do."

"Al," says Seni.

"Yeah," says I.

"Do you wanna finish this road trip, Al?" she asks.

I think, what is this? A trick question or something? I reply, "Well, yes, what do you think? I'm retired now. History. Finito.

Sign's down. Good-byes gifted, toasted, hands shaken and kissed off. That basically means I don't have nothing else to do, or anywhere else to go. I'm alone in the world now. Today is the first day of an extended vacation that will last until I die. Why else did I buy this rig? State of the goddamn art? Nineteen-hundred cubic feet of RV luxury. When you indians say let's go camping, then I mean I go camping . . . "

"No, really, Al. I mean sincerely, like a trip down memory lane. Heart and soul, Al. Like a spiritual journey, if you will?"

"Well, yeah, I guess, sure. Like a walk in the dark, right? OK, OK, just kidding," I hedge.

"Well, then, you better start to relax a little. Take a nap – I'll drive."

"I do look like shit, don't I?" I had to admit I fell flat on my face at my party last night. Drunk, but, hey, I do that whenever I try something new. See, there's a weeping series of stinging stitches on my left eyebrow, long scratches down the left side of my nose, and one hell of a bruised egg on my same-sex cheek. Har-dee-har-har.

OK, OK, maybe I am a bit hyper diaper. I can give up the driver's seat. Or I can rise to the occasion, so to speak – a fat white guy with all this dough, looking for the meaning of life. His life in particular.

See what I mean? Ah well, what does an old faggot like me know anyway? Just one more very confused, pitiful old man, four hundred and ten miles farther down the road, being driven into the trailer park, past the big ol' blinking neon sign with a big ol' rose on it, says, Rosalie's Flower Garden, next door to Meeko's Japan Girls.

I tell Seni to park my RV in front, where nobody is going to miss it. It's a warm evening. Irma comes out. High-slit tight skirt. Garters. Dark latina carrying a lap dog in each hand. Lips so red and thick and gooey, you just want to smear it all over your body.

"Al. Seni," she screeches, "Jeez, man, you really did come. I'd never 'ave believed it."

My eyes rake over her, because that's exactly what I'm supposed to do. Her legs spread apart, on those teensy-weensy, darling, bedroom, bound, slippered feet. Arms akimbo, hips a-pompom, she nuzzles past me like a llama on tippy-toes. I get a whiff of all that heady woman scent. She is looking at the RV, pokes fun at me.

"Jeez, Al, I thought the whole point of retirement was to lighten up a bit."

"Very funny, little girl," I reply irritably. She follows me in and snoops into every little nook and cranny.

"Jeez, man!" she exclaims. "You sure can feet a lot of bodies and stuff in there, eh?"

By now I am surrounded by girl bodies, one on each arm, cloying, warm, sheer, pink, baby, dolly, muses. Rosalie's style stayed in the nineteen-fifties. Showpiece low riders with white-wall tires and cadillac fins parked in plain view. Low white picket fences holding back the riot of asters everywhere. Neat, sanitized, wood-frame, auto court. Window boxes. The desert dust obsessively swept off the driveways and walkways thrice daily. Water is scarce, but she still has to have clipped green lawn, like throw rugs, under gleaming white lawn chairs, just for show. The calendar girls keep tumbling off the wall.

Then the kids crawl out. Lots of brown children and red chickens from the back compounds. They have figured out that I am not business, and they want to see too. Rosalie's kids are always clean, well fed, as perfectly groomed as their stage moms can get them, bullying the in-house hairdresser, insistent that their Liisa's hair look like that picture in the magazine. Well-loved, protected six-year-olds, all with their own gap-tooth innocence intact. To them I was other, and other has all sorts of possible meaning for them. A fat man means candy, cigarettes, rye whiskeys, gold watches inscribed with "Happy retirement, Al."

Irma's mouth hasn't stopped flapping since I arrived. She's figured out a use for every goddamn inch of my vehicle. I know that tex-mex mishmash lingo better than she thinks. I'm not that other. She's already checked out the goddamn engine. Then, as if she's just noticed, she comes sidling up to me.

"Hey, Al," she says, "this is some special day. Our baby dolly, Seni, comes back. Big daddy, you come back. Whaddya think? Lulu'd've been so proud of us. Rosie's gone to town for supplies for our big bonfire fete. She'll be back soon. Ooh, we going to have us some serious fun! 'Ey, you seen the hot tub yet? Ya gotta try it out, Al."

So I'm partying in the hot tub with the moon in my wineglass, and one of those forever and ever starry nights over our heads, and I'm laughing. Seni on my lap. Irma playing with her lap dogs, ignoring an asian whey-faced chit of a girl passing by with a chore or two, pouting at me and complaining, "That Irma. She's always the least funnest mom."

Rosalie, with her raucous laughter, saying, "Eh, Al, you still remember when you and Lulu bought this ol' trailer park, and Lulu convinced Irm and me to get off the strip to come work here. I remember I took one look at the four miserable trailers parked in the middle of nowhere, and I thought you two were nuts. No way I'd have stayed if it weren't for Irma . . . "

Irma adding, "The only reason I hung around wuz because you and Lu were nice. I've got a feel for people, you know. And you two were really nice. Dumb but nice. Who'd have ever thought that we'd be so blessed, eh?"

Seni piping in, "Well, I've still got my original shares. Al, you don't even have one little secret share left?"

I answering, "No way. Lulu made me promise that I'd sell out as soon as the business got on its feet. How about that

Lulu? If the place boomed, I got the boot. But if it went bust, I was allowed to stay. I swear that woman would've stole the shirt right off my back just for the show of it."

"Yeah, but when it comes to show people, you're the best, Al," comments Rosalie.

"She kept you humble, Al," adds Irma.

"To Lulu. And all her girls. And to many more generations of Lulu's girls," cries Seni, and we all solemnly toast Lulu, wherever she may be.

Next morning I am told that we're on our way into Mimbres Pass to dig the biggest barbecue pit we can. Then we're going to get high on life, and all dance like wild savages around the biggest fire we can build. And I am as excited as a two-year-old.

"But, Al," Rosalie teases, "we do this practically every other week. Not usually so far away, but Mimbres Pass is the most beautiful spirit place. High up on a mesa. We're going to celebrate the release of your spirit, Al. Your retirement, and Seni's health . . . Lulu's good work . . . our new hot tub . . . Joe's daughter, Violetta's pregnant . . . Can you imagine me a grandmother? Who'd ever have thought? Heck, Al, we sure do have a lot to be happy about."

So, with nineteen-hundred cubic feet of the most up-to-date RV luxury, packed by Irma with cages of live and therefore shitty chicken, a side of beef, which, oddly enough, did not "feet" in the refrigerator and had to go in the shower, sacks of rice, braids of garlic, necklaces of dried chili peppers, a kindergartenful of eerily well-behaved children, Seni and I happily start up the wagon train. I look over at her sitting beside me, and I can't help admiring how very grown up she has become.

"I once asked Lulu to marry me." I sneak a confession in. "You know, just for show. It was one of those times when I was dead broke, bankrupt to smithereens. What do you think she answered?"

"She said no, of course," Seni answers, "because the only model for relationships on the planet today is dominance and submission. And it's not just when a man and a woman get together. It's everywhere – this inequality that splits humanity. Right?"

"No, she said, 'Why, yes, of course, thank you very much, Al.' "

"Get outta here."

"OK, she said, 'Wife, kids, just another set of slaves, Al. You certainly have enough of those, don't you?' "

"Aha! My point exactly."

"So why don't you marry me for my money, Seni. I'm nobody without someone to boss."

Anyway, there was this old indian woman sitting on a folding lawn chair by an empty stretch of the highway like she was waiting for us, and nobody else. When she saw us, she waved us down and folded up her chair. I naturally slowed down, stopped and she hopped in. I mean, with everything else I've loaded up on, why not this one too? After a while, I ask Seni, "Well, who is she?" Because I thought she knew her.

"I don't know," Seni says. "You picked her up, so I thought you knew her."

"She got in here, waving and yapping and smiling at you as though you and she were good ol' friends," I say.

"She was waving and smiling at you too, Al."

"Goddamn!" was all I could say. You know, in my line of business, I'm supposed to be able to spot a phony a mile off. As a result, I think I see phonys everywhere. So what's the point? The point is I don't have one. Point no point. Who the hell ever does know where they're headed?

I'm not that old a guy. Fifty-three years old isn't old, but these days it's pretty worn out. And then that goddamn heart surgeon, and his exact words that if I don't start living soon, then I'll probably be dead in a couple of years really sliced through me! Not only was I going to die, but he tells me I never had a life to begin with. Supposedly it's not what you do but why you do it that really counts in the end. Motive is everything. In life. And murder mysteries. So why'd'ya do it, Al? Why d'ya murder yourself?

So, I think, maybe it's time to look back down the snaky, gravelly, oftentimes washboard road I've taken to get to where I am now. It runs for red rock mesa miles off the beaten track, and on it is a steady stream of sedans, vans and pickups, driven by shabby men, hooting, speeding, passing, kicking dust into each other's faces. Not in mine, of course – I have always had filtered air conditioning, while I drive my big hulking frame to where it doesn't fit so easily.

I was a blue-eyed, beautiful blond baby boy too. Grew up in the southern California suburbs with a smiling, albeit doped-up, simpering mommy, a small-town, lawyer-tyrant daddy and three lovely siblings. We are all good friends still, on and off. They, being realtors, Toyota salesmen, and high school teachers, still shake their heads over tall weekend screwdrivers under patio umbrellas, and say, "That Al," over and over again. They're awed that I, the ba ba black sheep of the family, swim in moneyed water way over their heads.

They used to hurt me. In fact, they tried to kill me. I guess they thought I went too far, broke too many of their mediocre rules, and they kind of took it personally. Hey, I could have hidden out in that safe, white, married zone. Appearances are everything. I knew that, but I was such a pretty boy, I never gave it a second thought. I did whatever I wanted to do. And I wanted to hang out with other pretty boys and play their other worldly games.

My downfall was when I fell in love with a black man. At first I was having so much fun working and playing with Mikey

I didn't notice when even my so-called peers turned on me. Sure, Al. You can't be serious. Har-dee-har-har. You can fuck 'em but that's all, man. Har-dee-har-har.

It turns out that I didn't fit in with them either. Too narrow. Too invested in their nigger games. Too mean. The territory of white male supremacy comes with all that defensiveness. To be honest, I was always so much better at those manoeuvres than they were anyway, so what did I have to goddamn prove.

I pass a road sign that says Truth or Consequences. Beyond it, scrub brush, blackbrush, sagebrush clump and bump and lump over a vast expanse of plains and valleys, and beyond them, pinyon-juniper forests straggle against the distant hills made flame red by the late-afternoon sun.

Seni stirs. When she looks over at me, she knows right away. Sometimes, it just gets too damn hard to go on.

"Do you want me to drive, Al?" she asks.

"No, I want you to tell me how to get beyond the pain." In spite of myself, my words snag on themselves.

Seni blinks. "You forgive yourself first." Her words are so gentle but they topple me.

Mikey, alias Mike Mann and the Mercy Mees, was the brilliant, black boy with a voice that breezed through the tight harmony of his throbbing love songs like tinkling leaves. And I was the bewitched white boy who was going to be a big cheese in show biz. Really, there was nothing to stop us from shooting right to the top. All I wanted was for him to get off his knees so I could worship him. And all he wanted was for me to get down on my knees to worship him. Before he destroyed himself, he snapped at me, his face black with rage, "You either peddling or fucking our asses, man. You a real big hero, aren't you, Al?"

"Did he hate me that much, Seni?" I ask like a beggar now.

"No, Al." She is trying to appease me. "It wasn't really him talking. It was the uppers and downers and the black beauties we were all riding day and night back then, Al. I was the same way. A winning white guy like you was just an easy target. We're all a little more grown up now, I hope."

"Anyone who blows his brains out just to show me doesn't want to grow up, Seni. You know how cheated I felt. Can you tell me, did he goddamn hate me that much?" I find I am actually yelling.

"No, he didn't hate you, Al. What can I say? Al, Al, you poor hurt boy, he was just having a stupid bad day that day, you know?"

Yeah, I guess I know, but can I feel it? I wonder. Can I feel anything genuine any more? What poor bugger should be made to suffer dead lovers upon retirement? What can one say about dead love anyway? You're merrily driving along and you see them. Road kills on the ten-lane freeways of life, battered, squashed, futile, wasted. Dot. Dot. Dot. Still life. Landscape washes. Canyon surrounds. Wild things tend to die early, I guess. They're like those dead ends in life; I drive into them still.

Farther down the road, when I calm down a little, I tell Seni about the Mercy Mees. All the years I have bent over backward to find work for this crowd. Thank goodness they were a good stage act and people never tired of their sleek, black patent american clichés. Mind you, without Mikey they never did another album, but they never seemed to get old in their fur-trimmed suits neither. They limousined contentedly about town, languished backstage. And I have always treated them like stars, kept up with their boy troubles and various suburban sundry.

"Al, after all these years, you are still just a yankee doodle boy," says Seni, laughing at me.

"But I'm not the enemy, Seni." And that, it seems, was the best I had left to offer.

We pull into a gas station to fill up on gas and propane, and three tubs of ice cream. Hey, kids are supposed to like ice cream.

Of course another one of those proud, retired RV owners had to come up and compare chassis notes with me. He finds himself staring at Mrs. Old Lady Yellow from the side of the road, a sun-dried, raisinlike, squat, wrinkled elder from the somewhere unpronounceable chapter house, with the grey felt hat on her head and her buffalo-bladder pouch of sacred red dust on her lap, dozing in the front swivel captain's chair. The guy's curious about her presence in this sleek interior. He's trying to decide – indian art or not.

"Mother-in-law," I sheepishly explain. You know, just to get a rise out of him. He looks as if he needs a good curio or two to share with his wife.

"Family," I say humbly, referring to the lineup of serious little brown faces peeking out the windows. I watch him go, watch his slim, trim, upright, uptight rear end head back into the convenience store, wondering why I'm the one always made to feel like shit. I felt like yelling, Hey, fella, you should see the little lady, because here comes Seni, bellydancing her way along in a summery white halter dress, cinched at the waist. Her earlobes and toes decorated with bunches of plastic fruit, her arms full of peaches and cream. As she goes by, she flashes a pinup smile at the guy and he falls over the curb and like drops dead.

So much later, in the dark ruptured moonscape around us, all my good ol' friends, dead or alive, get up and dance. Slow shuffling cold feet at first, we all keep our self-conscious distance from the hot orange fiery centre of our soulful songs. But before long, we heat up with fire in our veins. We forget ourselves and throw off our chains. I see arms and faces float up into the night, following the rise of thousands of flaming sparks from our huge cackling bonfire. Intoxicating smoke from burning pinyon and juniper wood makes my eyes tear. The world transforms itself into blurred, swirling shapes, eerie, ghostlike, outlines flickering, deceiving, suddenly effaced by darkness.

And Seni's erotic dance begins with the teasing twitch of tassels and the scented swish of her skirt's edge. The tinkling of small talk; peals of laughter. Suddenly the air gets detonated by the booming explosion of a dozen jar drums. She twirls around and shakes out amazing magic, scattering power – sometimes soft, pliant flutters of spiritual calm, oftentimes pounding purges. I want her to go on and on forever. And they do, these extravagant feelings of unbearable pleasure that make me want to roll in the dust and tear my throbbing heart out of my chest for all the world to view.

The exquisite wafting sounds of reeded flute and zills played together, echoing along canyon rock. The tingling of little hairs on the back of my neck makes me crazy. I want to break down. I want to cast away my weary little life. I strain to reach into the huge grotesque shadows just below the surface of consciousness. I want to conjure them up and fling them onto the ground, shrieking and twisting, so they have no more power over me. I scream and stomp and watch them waver and stagger and fall into chaos. Only new beginnings can follow an act like that.

Comes the next morning, Seni and I lie out in the hot sun. I smile into the blinding sunlight and close my eyes to feel the eternity of this moment. I can relax now, because I have finally arrived here and now. My flesh is melting away in great gobs and hunks. Earlier, a small child needed her shoelaces tied, so she came to the nearest grown-up and pointed her tippy-toe at me. I reached over and did it before I even realized that I could do it. I have lost, or given away, or thrown out a lot of the baggage that I used to exhaust myself with. As a result, I was feeling giddy and light-headed and alive.

"Please, Al," Seni groans, "for god's sake, what do you want to know for? There's no meaning in these stories. We just tell them to pass the time."

"Seni, darling, we're all living just to pass the time. And you're just saying that because you think that no one will question what is meaningless. But that makes your meaninglessness all the more questionable, doesn't it?"

"Oh my god!" She giggles, and covers her face with her pretty straw hat. "OK, you're kind of close to understanding but you're not quite there yet." She playing games.

"What, what? Tell me again." I am such a sucker for peekaboo, and I love to hear her laugh.

"I can't. You gotta find out for yourself. It's hard work, and it feels mental."

"I'm not afraid of being mental. Just tell me what to do."

"Al, in fact you work like mad to avoid the real work of feeling mental."

"Aah," I sigh. "So this is fate for old shits like me. To go around chasing hot little girls for quickie answers. And not getting them."

"All right, I'll tell you what I know, but that is really all I know about Lulu. In Spain, in that plasticized tourist trap you sent us to, Al, these flotsam people started crawling out of the woodwork at Lulu. They were different from the rest of the vacationers. All frayed and rickety, glasses taped together, greying hair, and it wasn't that they looked poor, because some were not. It was more that they had the same ghostly expression of people who were heavily addicted to their past.

"One night, some old guy drank too much, called himself a freedom fighter and said to me, 'In the old days, we loved our artists, you know, but the fascists . . . they knew exactly what to destroy first.'

"Remember how at first Lulu was so excited about going

back to Europe, but then she started to drink heavily again. I think she lost something very big over there. According to this guy, she was supposedly a member of the Ka family, rich and famous for generations. Her grandfathers, great-grandfathers owned incredible circuses all over Europe. They were either jews and their enemies hated them for being gypsies, or they were actually gypsies and people thought they were jews. I can't remember which. First the Black Shirts murdered the uncle. Then the rest of the family were ambushed and gunned down at his funeral. I imagine Europe was a pretty fun place in her day. Anyway, whoever was left either got arrested or they disappeared in other discreet ways."

"She told me she was italian" – I offered what I knew – "and lived in a convent until it got blown up in the war. Then she came to America by marrying a G.I. They were farmers in Idaho for years and years, until he died in a tractor accident, and his brothers got everything. And she told Mike that she was an orphan, bellydanced her way through life when times were good, sucked a lot of cock when times were bad."

"Yeah, well, maybe it's all true, Al. Let her go. The way I figure it, there are plenty more Lulus all over this world."

"Then I guess we'll never know," I said, disappointed. "You can't have any kind of ending if you don't even have a beginning, can you?"

"Well, we do have another story. It's a very old story, and it comes from an old book that Lulu left me."

"What kind of story?" I pop up, ever hopeful.

"Well, if you really think about it, any kind of story will do, Al . . ."

Goddamn, that Seni never misses a trick.

". . . but if you really want to know, Al, then turn the page."

POMPEII

MY GREAT-GRANDMOTHER used to tell a story of an ancient woman who could look into her body as if it were a deep well and pull out many secrets about herself. And others. Great-grandmother said that the well woman was a part of a tribe of mountain people who were just born like that. Before their people melted away, they had stories of how they came to be. Their goddesses came to their very stony country in a nutshell. None of them could survive in their harsh surroundings, but a daughter was born to them. She was different and could live. She married a mountain god and, in turn, started an ancient lineage of women who could bare only daughters.

"And quite decidedly *bare* not *bear,* as fully human women do. Oh, they became human, but not quite enough," said the great-grand, her hands gloved in coarse flour, as she pointed and spoke this story, as she patted and twisted the dough that became, and never soon enough, sweet dumplings for me, my sisters, my younger aunties and my cousins – all girls. Kneeling in front of her summer hide house, she squinted at the sun receding behind western mountains and added, "Never quite. With such beginnings, they turned out to be a strange, wayward tribe of women. They had to be captured into marriage and raped to breed. And many died gruesome deaths, because they fought against the cycle of their human lives. In order to birth their babies, their bulging bellies had to be slit, and the fruit popped out of the dying mother like dragon eyes."

I was too young to know death. My small chirping mouth watered at the mention of juicy dragon eyes, a rare delicacy. My little plump hands rolled out the balls of sweet seed paste faster than Iron Ways Girl, faster than Sublime Life Journey, faster than any of my cousins, and dropped them into the great flat woven pans to our great-granny's praise. Behind me, our aunties pounded the seed and root into paste. Dorje lovingly added honey – lots of honey. "More honey, Auntie!" we greedy young ones used to cry out with such giggling.

Remembering this story of my great-grandmother, I stare out to sea – not quite weeping, just the edges of my vision moistened. Today is a beautiful day – just not warm. It is the fish-swarming season. Many people are fishing off the rocks. It can be very risky. And I have seen many fall in. Some crawl back up the crags and jags. Others sink beneath the surging, foaming surf as if they were never there. But I do not wail like some others. These are not my people now.

Besides, I have stood out there myself. I know what it is to be afraid and not afraid in the midst of the thundering. Naked, drenched with thick ocean spray, I have shuddered in the sharp wind and danced to keep a raw warmth within me. One by one the biggest, greediest fish came to me. I lured them in and clubbed them to death. I passed them on to those who were my people then, waiting, hungry, who cheered me on.

I have won a lot this way. That is the reason I still come here to watch. And to remember. See there, far away, on that submerged tip – you can barely see it. That is where my childishly thin body once stood my fragile ground. You know, I did not need Neptune's trident to poke and prod. I did not have to swing wet, weighted nets off slimy edges. And I did not half submerge myself in the surf, dipping with grass baskets, or reach with pitifully bare hands, as the poorest, hungriest women and children did. They were the ones most easily swept away.

Instead, I cleverly baited a wickedly devised hook. See how small, how easy, how like an ear bauble it is? I still wear it as a reminder many times over, to wait unafraid after I cast out my lure. Except the point no longer pierces as it used to, and the leather strap has rotted off. It was given to me by a merchant who was rich and my first lover. Before he went away, he told me that with this small sliver of metal I need never starve. I cried bitterly – silly, girlish that I was. Oh, how I curse that one now for opening up a huge, gaping, yawning, greedy black hole in one so young, so soulfully young. He – in fact, they have all, upon their leave – blithely tossed me the hard glinty choice to stay alive or not. Yes, indeed, I've had the hook dipped in silver and now I wear it embedded in the flesh of my breast. And, no, it doesn't hurt any more.

Today, as I do every year during the time of the swarming of the fish, I keep my pact to meet on these rocks, but there are so few of my relatives left. And even those still alive have conveniently forgotten. They are pampered matrons now, and their daughters marry rich. They loll in their lush peristyles, caressing their slaves with one hand as they torture with the other, being freed women themselves. They no longer venture beyond the city walls to sit on hard rocks and shiver in the wind if it turns out to be windy, or cower in the rain if it rains, or get scorched by the sun if it turns out to be sunny.

Neither do they want to remember who we are, or how we came to live here, or the days when we worked and never stopped. Woke at dawn, running, toiling, gathering. We sacrificed the fish, slit their wriggling bellies and clawed the life out of them. Peddlers, hagglers, cajolers we were. Laughing at the feel of roman coins on our palms. Stinking of fermented fish sauce, living new lore.

And old ones – oh, I remember. I still talk to our old ones. If the others sought out the old ones' counsel, they wouldn't act the way they do. My relatives have renamed themselves Lucretia and Ariadne, and me Lulu.

"Lulu," they say, "you're too old-fashioned."

"Don't you call me Lulu," I say fiercely. "My name is Dance of the Eternal Spirit. It is one thing to give them a name to call you. And quite another to become the slave name that is not you."

"Shh, the slaves will hear. Look, we're not barbarians any more," they hiss at me.

When I hear this, I shake my head in sorrow and say, "Shame, shame. You have let them shame you."

"Dance of the Eternal Spirit, you won't be able to get back home, no matter how hard you try," they warn.

"I will get home," I answer fiercely, with all my heart.

I alone, it seems, have chosen not to live in the atrium of my master's house. I don't know if this makes them afraid for me, or afraid of me. Great-granny knows we were hardly slaves at all. But slavishness is all in the heart after all, isn't it? We were children – captive children. Even then, after the horror, I had a dagger in my hand, ready to plunge into my belly. My great-grandmother stopped me with her dying plea.

"No, my beauty, you cannot choose that way. It has been foretold, my darling, that you will live and go with them. Go down the mountain, child. You will see the sea."

That is how I left the remains of our most beloved, our ancient village and our ecstasy. In the pelting rain, and in chains, I looked back. Since then, Great-grandmother, I have travelled a great distance indeed! I have learned not to cling, because clinging hurts so much. And I have done anything I have needed to do to keep those chains from cutting too deep into my core. It took twenty-eight moons to get to this fucking town. And I do mean fucking. People come here to fuck and to relax. He, he, he.

We came in the year of what I call the rollicking times. Earthquake. It was rollicking for us girls, anyway. We came right afterward. The minute our boat scraped rock, our grooms, in fact the whole crew, leapt off the boat and went running to their broken houses. They weren't bad guys. They left the tigers unleashed in their cages and us to wander as we would. There were just ten of the toughest of us left.

And the town was in total chaos; the roman people were in total awe of the forces of nature, as they are so fond of mentioning. In other words, they were addicted to cheap thrills in their bloodthirsty arenas. Aah. But weren't they – weren't we all – just real fun people in a real fun time? And didn't that make us all slaves in this menagerie town?

When our hosts turned around and saw us wandering along their narrow streets, they were amazed. Of course they took the time to question us. We all spoke excellent empirical language by then. They were immediately charmed. We gathered a crowd wherever we went, and they pampered us like exotic monkeys. This bakery gave us baked bread and roasted nuts for breakfast. Another shop gave us wine for our work rebuilding altars and shrines. Rich ladies were already offering any combination of prices for us. But we ran off into the hills, where we slept under silver leaves in moonlit orchards.

At noontime, when the heat seemed to fall straight down from the heavens, we bathed in sparkling golden streams. Even young patricians used to run and dance day and night on the verdant hillsides among spring flowers, chased by pets, slaves and playmates. For the adventurous young, for a glorious moment, the earthquake levelled all differences. In the excitement of its aftermath, they pledged renewal to their most beloved slaves. They swore that one day the slaves would share their masters' ascendancy. And we laughed and laughed, because even then, as now, we knew we would never understand their lopsided kind of love.

But the citizens understood. We were just young girl slaves, after all, waiting on our master, who knew he could round us up any time he wanted. That was exactly it. There was nowhere to escape to. Every place would have been no place that we could have understood. In the beginning, when we were torn from our homelands, I etched in memory each and every place we passed so that I would never forget the way back. But that was before I realized the sheer magnitude of the extent of this very strange world. We were such innocents, captured at first, then captivated by our own desire to know. But ultimately we immured ourselves by our knowing much more than we ever should have.

And so seventeen years passed. Great-grandmother, forgive me, I have learned to count time like money, thereby losing my eternity. At first, I thought I had been trapped by circumstances – like this horrid little town specifically. But, no, in many ways, this place has graciously unshackled me and permitted me to make my own way in it. Only later did I realize that I had a further need, often despairing and violent, to unshackle myself, this being the essential difference between a free woman and a freed woman.

"And a lot more oppressive than the heat, don't you think, Senator?" You see, Great-grandmother, I have had to come to understand the importance of gesture. And it has paid off because now they are all very, very aware of whom I entertain at my cenas in this boring little last-resort town of middling managers, poets, senators, famous gladiatorials, self-professed prophets and . . . everywhere . . . soldiers on brain leave. Oh, sigh, one has to have the soldiers, though. They bring out the daughters, and that's good for business. Even the emperor's daughter, Julia. Wasn't that nice? An unofficial daughter, as I recall, but still when she came to my domus, this plebeian, unfinished hole-in-the-wall town hummed for a goodly while.

"My dear, dear, lovely hostess, I believe it's all in the unevenness," replied the drunk. "Of course unevenness can be extremely pleasing to the senses – a subtle snub here, a slight bump there, the bantering back and forth. Anything to relieve the monotony, but how easily it can get out of hand. Lulu, my turtle dove, will you dance for us tonight?" he demanded.

The evening certainly wasn't any evening in particular. Always the same conversation, the same performance, peals of laughter in the warm evening breeze, the trickle of the water fountain, musicians in the garden – the artful details of my summer triclinium were endless. Seven skilled cooks I had in my employ, forty slaves to light the oil lamps that kept the evening glowing, to pour the wine and spill the food, to run messages to and from the bath suites, to wipe greasy fingers, to bare some youthful flesh, to appease the satyric violence. But it was the night that Northern Star Gazer did not come, and after she had promised me just that morning, for jumpin' Jupiter's sake.

"Come dance your slow and wispy dance for me tonight, my love," I had wheedled at her, lovingly holding her reflection in her silver mirror for her to see. "The greek royal and his very undistinguished entourage will surely come if you dance, and they're the social catch of this achingly dull week."

She smiled at me as the morning lit up her pale hair and face.

"No," she teased, "I get into such trouble when I go into your establishment."

"That is because you don't do as I tell you," I reasoned.

"Oh, don't oppress me. Why should I do what anyone tells

me? I don't want for anything, but I know you. You're just like all the others. You all want to chomp on me," said she.

"Then don't go with them any more! Let me take care of you. I'd buy your way out of slavery, if you would only let me. Don't you want to be freed?" I was, as always, so determined, and seriously full of myself.

Northern Star Gazer threw her head back and laughed. "And you of all my demanding lovers want the most. Tell me, where is this way to freedom for you? You, who'll never be able to rest until your conquerors, all your conquerors – me included – have been put to death. Look in this moon-shaped mirror and tell me if clinging to the shit of your hatred doesn't make you blossom with beauty."

I remember I felt cold, dampened by an unusual morning mist, which had suddenly drifted over us. The reflection at which we both gazed darkened ominously.

"Even so, my darling, you will come and dance for my patrons, won't you?" I repeated it because it was true – I knew of no other way.

Her laughter reminded me of the children we once were, dangling like bats off a branch of a fig tree. It was then that Northern Star Gazer taught me to string dill in my hair. She was amazed by my black snake coils; I was amazed by her white silk tresses. She touched the texture of mine and laughed with pleasure at the strange braids. We kissed to taste each other.

"You were taken away as well?" she chattered like a flight of small birds. "I have not seen the likes of you and your cousins. Many of us come from the north. But only I come from the place of the white sister cliffs called Vercin. And I am going home soon. Lamia is a nubian from the sands to the south. She's a dancer, and she won't talk to you because she hates you."

I stole a peek at the sullen disagreeable giantess of a child who stabbed back with long vicious stares.

"Why does she hate me?" I asked brutally.

"Because she is hungry and dirty," Northern Star Gazer said blithely.

"Well, why doesn't she eat and wash?" was my supercilious suggestion.

"She does but it will always be so," she tweaked.

"We are all betting on how much you all will fetch. Have you ever had to drink the bring-on-the-cramps drink? So that a baby can't grow inside you. I had to drink it twice. It was awful, and I almost died. I'm only twelve. How old are you?"

Oh, by then I was always old and learning fast. We were children, and suddenly I was not. Lamia said it best in her own mutinous way.

"Rule number one – don't let them fuck you! That's all. Especially important for those of us who can't expect anything more."

Soon after that, Lamia was made to learn dance from her outcast people, and Northern Star Gazer, being the blonde that dark romans idolized, was taken in to learn how to submit genteelly to being worshipped, and I was sold into servitude, although I quickly bought myself out into the freedom of poverty on the streets, where I prudently learned to move fast. Yet we all continued to contrive little ways to come together, if only for a youthful moment.

But Lamia was forever getting caught and beaten. It was a wonder she did not break in two. Or did she?

"Lamia," I cried, always uneasy to see her in my tiny back-alley black hole of a shop, "you here again. Why do you come? Go back. I can't bear to see you beaten any more."

But at the time, she was so high and mighty, a disguise of powerlessness.

"Can you ever imagine why these romans so love to fill their ugly mugs with this putrid, between-their-buttocks fish stench.

Indeed, their very souls stink of it," she taunted and teased. "And, Dance of the Eternal Spirit, do you still believe you can buy your little slave way to spiritual freedom, smelling like that?"

"And sweet Lamia," I once ventured to ask, "don't you ever tire of being so much better than anybody else?"

There were moments, though, when she hung her bruised head and wept piteously, and I would gently tell her stories. "When I look at you, I see an oasis, an emerald jewel in a forever sea of ever-shifting sand, full of mirages and dreams. Do you feel it as well, Lamia? There, don't you see it? That was a place of ecstasy for you. It is your ancient home and it still holds a special place for you by its evening fire. You must remember. Tell me that you know what it is to grow up and old, surrounded by your own people, and to hear them contentedly droning out their ancient stories of the days and seasons that were eternal."

"I was born in captivity." Her reply wry and dry. "I have no memory of where I came from, and this is the reason that I can only stay brutishly in the present. Ask any one of my many dissatisfied mistresses. Are they not forever saying that there will be no future for the likes of me?"

Aah, but, Great-granny, my love Lamia's tears never lasted. Before I knew it, I would be at her mercy.

"Little one," Lamia said, "don't you think I have seen the many magnificent mountain people who were wild and untameable when they came here? Many died because they couldn't stop clinging to what is gone. And so . . . so they're dead. The best is dead. And life is short, and death is long. And so . . . so I say, come dance in the streets with me. It's boy-swarming time. Show those handsome young men your name."

"Oh, don't bother me," I said. "So much work, I cannot rest."

"You'll be able to make ten times the doggy scraps you earn catching fish. I can't bear to see your pedigree arms fermenting in this disgusting fish sauce. Come, my pet. Why do you resist? You're so tense because you know what I say is true. Come, and you shall have your dream of freedom. I too want it for you. I do, I really do. Wash first."

So we ran off to the plazas and squares – anywhere crowds gathered for evening pleasantries. There, Lamia threw me about and made me do whatever she required. She used to wrap her legs and body around me, pressing against me to unleash my suppleness, dousing me with her intoxicating scents and oils, murmuring erotically in my ear, as I straddled and slid meltingly down her long, strong and very slick thighs.

Our captivating stance reeked of plunder, and the citizens of the republic rather enjoyed that. We gained in notoriety. I got my riches, and Lamia kept laughing with loud raucous rancour. Indeed, if she ever did lie back and spread herself open with hips grinding and legs lasciviously held up, her admirers never knew whether they were going to haphazardly get in or get a treacherous kick in the head.

Then, there were the times when Lamia and I would go and torment Northern Star Gazer for her lack of ambition. On moonless nights, we crawled along tiled roofs until we dropped into her gardens. We didn't even have to be quiet, giggling to our hearts' content, for we knew well enough the wine-soaked sleep of romans. And for a cherished goddess like Northern Star Gazer, who was too valuable to squander on common fucking, her mistresses always added supplements of sleeping potions in her many paying guests' food and drink. And if potions were not persuasive enough, Lamia could be much more convincing. Being a big-boned girl, she'd pick each erstwhile perpetrator right out of Northern Star Gazer's bed and drop him out in the black-as-night back lane with the other wild dogs. And that, Great-grandmother, should have been that, if it weren't for the eternal fool of a girl, who has always insisted that she was never going to grow up.

"The both of you, leave me be!" she balked at what she felt was our petty-minded sabotage of her roman god-given privileges, stamping her pretty feet as hard as she could, "What is your problem, for Juno's sake? He says he loves me. He's tender with me. And he's rich. And I want to be his slave. Look at this silk he bought me. Endless lengths of such softness you have never felt."

"It's not enough. Not for what you go through. It's really dumb the way you let them fuck you to death, Northern Star Gazer. You risk your own life, and Lamia and I aren't going to let you kill yourself now, are we?" We learned to manoeuvre skillfully around her as though she were a puma in heat, praying for what we knew was inevitable.

"Oh, he's gone." The same stupid sobbing songs over and again, her head buried in Lamia's lap while I stroked her comfortingly. "He's left me for another. But I can't live without him. I'm nothing without him. I want to tear my heart out for him. I shall cut it into little pieces to show him . . . "

Oh, but she could dance. Wouldn't you know that it would be Northern Star Gazer who carried the most fearsome force. The mistresses all believed that she held sacred underworld power, for many witnessed it erupt without warning through her earthly body; and they would have made her a high priestess if she was not just a slave – and a terribly ambivalent one at best.

People come to this town in droves, seeking their myths. Every other roman day is a time for ritual and feasting. I remember one particular festival of descent into death and rebirth into light. After the parade up the mountain where sheep and pigs and cakes and seed and fruit were thrown into the groaning sometimes belching cracks in the earth, they all came down to watch Northern Star Gazer and other magicians perform miracles. I never understood it myself, watching these romans all astir as if so anxious to feel their own sense of helplessness in front of their gods.

I was one of those allowed to serve and observe from the fringes, and Lamia was one of those hired to pulsate around the mosaic-and-myrrhed roomful of drunken guests with serpents and things. I remember waiting. I was wearing an awful short tunic and pouring endless trickles of wine until my arms almost fell off. I was disgusted by the smell of vomit and urine, but I too waited nervously for one of Northern Star Gazer's pure expressions when she would rise like pale wispy smoke from the altar fires – her eyes unblinking and transfixed by a throbbing climax within her. In the flickering shadows, an apparitional light glowed from her breast. She threw her head back, exposing her long white throat in a swanlike swoop, and began strange little strangulated cries of distress.

And I was swatting groping hands off my butt when I suddenly saw Lamia surge through the air – her huge glossy body quivering with lust and hunger. She pounced on all fours on top of Northern Star Gazer, who was forced down into a soft and pliant, kneeling back bend. She held in limbo with her eyes wide open in a bloodless esctasy. For an instant I felt sick and faint because I saw with my own disbelieving eyes Lamia's carnal fangs sink deep into her flesh.

I pulled back, recovering in time to hear the crowd murmur its appreciation of Northern Star Gazer and Lamia dancing together. Their chiaroscuro beauties seemed to innocently follow one another. Pink and tawny ankles flying to the breathless tempo of flutes, and the wild panting of drums, reaching and maintaining a seemingly impossible pitch, while my heart pounded with an unknown fear. I glanced around, confused about what had happened. What was that vision so astonishing?

Later, Lamia, all upside down and beside herself, claimed that Northern Star Gazer had given her back her panther spirit. And that was when I remembered as well. Yes, I told her, Northern Star Gazer can do that. She helped me travel home in a trance once. Just once. We were so young I thought we were just kidding around. I could not have done it myself, but we doubled the power within us, and I awoke in the sweet tall grass of my clan village's nearby meadow.

My first thought was how did the grass get so tall? But of course there were no more goats to graze it, no more hands to hay it. I waded through the long grass towards my great-grand-mother's house, and almost immediately became exasperated and confused. I never remembered grass like this. It got in the way of everything. It snagged my limbs, and I had to beat it down. I got so angry I burst into tears.

The house was still there, though there was something dras-tically missing from its familiar. It seemed to be hiding from me or preventing my approach. And I couldn't find a way to pass the place where I knew I had left the broken body of our great-grandmother. In life she was always honoured with the silkiest robes, the finest embroidery, the softest hides and rich-est furs, but in death, stripped by the marauders, like a half-skinned carcass on muddy half-frozen ground. How wrong it felt to not be able to prepare her passage. How hatefully, horri-bly inhuman.

I looked and looked but I couldn't find a trace of her. Not one collar bone. Or anyone else for that matter. But that hadean grass really got to me. I looked down and saw that I was drenched in its sticky dew, covered with its tiny seeds and almost smothered by its cloying pollen. I collapsed with a nau-seous feeling of unremitting clawing at the base of my belly and fought deliriously to get back up.

I awoke in Northern Star Gazer's arms. Her then-young woman's face broke wide open with relief. She said that she almost couldn't bring me back.

"Your grannies must have helped," she added excitedly, her eyes as big and endless as bowls of blue sky. She was shaken by the amazing thing we did together. I was flat-out sick for three days.

Since then I have pretended that I had forgotten. I had to lie, whenever she asked, you see, because it was too much for me to go to that place. As many times as I craved it, I was too afraid, not only for me, but for Nothern Star Gazer especially. It looked like home, but it felt like demons within. And every slave dreams of freedom, without knowing all that it possibly can be.

I have always known that it was too easy for Northern Star Gazer to slip effortlessly into her diaphanous trances, where she felt calm and infinite while her body wilted and sickened. I also knew she didn't have the substance I had to fight her way back. Indeed, she wouldn't have wanted to come back from her beloved childhood in Vercin.

The night she would not come to dance, I was put out and sent messages, but she did not reply. I thought that I already knew why, but for once she tricked both Lamia and me.

"Have this baby, then." I remember my voice rising at her like the wind before a storm. "Just go ahead and have it!" What was so terrible about that? Wasn't a slave's meagre pledge to life better than nothing at all? Well, wasn't it? Why, it could have been a free-born daughter. I could have easily arranged it. Our own beautiful little girl with rosebud lips and a violet tiara in her soft curls.

She didn't have to drink that poison. She chose that way, perhaps because she knew the risks too well. By the time her distraught servants came to fetch me, the last of my paying guests had careened off. It was early morning, the first glimmer of light in the east, and Northern Star Gazer was dying in a ring of blood. So fast, I thought in slow motion, so soon. And here I had always thought that because I loved her so much, she would naturally want to stay with me. I lifted her in my arms. She smiled her fond little smile and quietly refused all my lavish gifts of life.

She left me here, trapped in time, a very long time, staring out to sea. Lamia is also gone. Early one morning she and this trader and his caravan eloped through the southern gate. I went to see her off, hoping that she'd change her mind and stay with me. She kissed me good-bye instead, and said, "I just have to go. If I stay here, I know I'm going to get buried alive."

"Aren't you scared, Lamia?" I yelled after her silhouette in the twilight dusk of dawn.

"Beyond words, my darling," she cried, "but that's life, isn't it?"

So what choice did I have except to go deep into the secret well of my body. There, I float about its dark waters. There, it occurred to me that Northern Star Gazer's dance was of death just as Lamia's dance was of life. And my dance, Great-grand-mother, was the hardest, needed the most skill and endurance and was still the clumsiest. Mine is a chaotic dance that tries to embrace both life and death, that gets played over and over again, that must be danced in terrible solitude. Moreover, I have always thought that I grovelled the most.

Indeed, evening winds are picking up. And still none of the relatives come. Curse their sloth anyway. I need my cloak of silk and a little more wine. I have some youngsters roasting a juicy red fish on a spit in front of me. I like to watch their vim and fire against the brilliant pink and purple hues of sunset. My slaves entertain me with double flutes and cymbal.

Geta, a retired centurion, had generously offered me the use of his lyre and the amazing slave who plays it. Regrettably I had to decline both, because I knew Geta would make up any excuse to come with them. And today has turned out to be my day to meditate alone – something a roman legionary would probably not understand.

Around me the hillsides are dry and wrinkled. The barley fields finished, now bare. Even the trusty umbrella pine trees look tired and droopy. In my youth, sunsets were very sudden – massive rock mountains cast long, chilled shadows into our daily lives, and the grandmothers hurried up their chores so that they could start the evening rituals. These, according to memory, were warm, cosy, childlike songs in front of a glowing home fire.

I get up because I cannot wait for those who no longer care. Standing to let fall the graceful folds of my gown, I feel the little tremors in the earth. My girl slave scrambles out of her sleep. I never scold; I wait until she lifts the rod of the umbrella high enough to protect me. I have my veils as well. Then we proceed along the road built of stone, lined with tall thin cypresses, like pointy paintbrushes slowly colouring in the rich indigo of evening. My embroidered sandals step in time to the lonely, lilting wailing of flutes. With the leftover heat of the day stirring in the tall grass, crickets fire up high-pitched songs with their wings. My hips start to sway and swing lovingly to the cadence of the cymbals. My slaves and the poor children of the streets hop and skip and twist and cavort around me. I lift my hands in salutes of peace to my people who will surely come again. They are not far away, I know. Hardly a day or night goes by without the ancient ones telling me many wonderful things about the home to the east that waits patiently for me.

Then I notice my great-grandmother's soft moon face serene and high above some fretful flashes of lightning along the distant horizon line of mountains. On this oddly restive August night, I know I will gaze up at her from my bed and feel her silvery love for me as I close my eyes.

THE SOONG
SISTERS

UNTIL THEY GOT THEIR eviction notices, Sue Mei, May Lynn, and Su-lin were bickering as usual. At the time, the argument was about Su-lin's old beans in the rooftop garden. And that, of course, got batted along to other points of contention, such as May Lynn's good-for-nothing, mangy old carpet of a dog. But none of this was all that serious. May Lynn and Su-lin, who do most of the spatting and batting, still slept with their apartment doors open – the summer evenings being hot and humid, and the Vancouver of 1972, which Sue Mei contemplated from the top of their four-storey apartment building, being quiet and peaceful. Up the street, the many-splendoured neon lights of chinatown were as yet the brightest flowers of the night.

When the notices to evict actually arrived in the post, Sue Mei was sitting at May Lynn's kitchen table, eating the crappiest things for breakfast. Instant coffee. Waffles that tasted like their cardboard box, swimming in a toxic brown puddle of corn syrup, smeared with margarine kept in a greasy, plastic yellow container with its printed label flaking off. And reading the local newspaper, swallowing it like a daily source of disgruntlement. The ink on the newsprint comes off, but the stories decidedly do not, was her predictable complaint. May Lynn sipped herbal tea, reading the *Manchester Guardian*. Her mutt smelled old and doggy. But this was perhaps not the time for Sue Mei to mention that again, because May Lynn paid for all the newspaper subscriptions, and the good ol' morning sun does shine through once in a while.

By the time the notion of eviction arrested their attentions, these grey framed envelopes from the powers-that-be – i.e., governments and banks – were becoming less and less a curiosity. After all, hadn't they all three once successfully tackled the omnipotence of the passport office for their journey back to their ancestral villages near Hoy Saan? Sue Mei claimed that if they could do that, they could do anything. She had done all the talking for them to the perfunctionary at the wooden counter, referring to the trip as their travels abroad. A few years ago, that seemed quite the occasion, for which she took her fur coat out of storage and unwrapped her snap-top, black leather purse. (These days, Sue Mei grumbled bitterly about the diminishing quality of life. Woodward's beautiful food floor was kaput. She trudged over to the Dollar Meat Market in worn-out sneakers and tacky sweat pants, and she, too, kept her change purse in a pocket sewn into her waistband.)

"We're being evicted," offered Sue Mei to the everlasting, boring calm of the tiny kitchen nook with its faded yellow arborite, its hobbled and chipped table; to the plastic squeeze bottles; to the cracked cups drying in the drainer, to the ten thousand years of soot on the outside of the window that overlooked the regurgitating garbage bins in the alley.

May Lynn's mouth dropped open. Then they both turned their heads and yelled simultaneously out the door, down the hall to Su-lin's apartment, where she was probably feeding her cagefuls of rats and mice, cooing at the little horrors like beloved children.

"Suuuee weee," they mimicked without giggles this time, "Suee weee." Until they heard Su-lin's slippers shuffling along the creaking linoleum floor, slapping out a slavish rhythm. Until her lovely face popped around, looking for goodies.

But then there was no sense in mentioning the eviction notices until Su-lin got settled. She'd have to test the fading warmth of the teapot, or get an extra plate or sniff at the instant coffee in Sue Mei's cup first. Oh, and here come those leechy cats of hers, thought Sue Mei cattily! Oh, and even better, the snoop from downstairs, nicknamed Madame Cabbage Face!

"Chou Taitai was nice enough to come and visit." Su-lin smiled at Madame Cabbage Face, who had followed her across the threshold, only to be abruptly shoved back out by Sue Mei. But wasn't this kind of brutish behaviour expected of Sue Mei? Chou Taitai and she have had words before. One squawk more or less hardly makes a difference in this shitty henhouse, Sue Mei had once told her in a livid snit, but today she took some pains to be nice.

"Oh, then perhaps Chou Taitai would be kind enough to come back another time? Because we have private business to attend to," she said and closed the door.

"What business?" asked Su-lin, who was looking for pet food and hardly listening. At their feet there were some rumblings because May Lynn's dog did not get along with Su-lin's cats. And Sue Mei was feeling very pressured by now.

"We got eviction notices," blurted out Sue Mei. Aah, finally, the appreciative silence that she very much needed to hear.

Days later, Sue Mei found herself groping through decades of dust in the closet and thinking mournfully, Aah, life is but a passing dream. Nothing fit her any more.

"What on earth do they wear these days?" she asked May Lynn, even though she knew that nothing had really changed except her way of looking at things but, as a result, everything has changed. And, of course, May Lynn was no help.

"Sue Mei, for god's sake," she said, exasperated. "You think it matters to them what you wear? Those greedy buggers are hoping we show up wearing a coffin as soon as is convenient. Anything less is incidental. Hey, if you really want to make a big splash, go naked and fart in their ugly mugs. That ought to get their attention, love. Go as stark raving naked as you seem to feel."

All Sue Mei found was an old suitcase full of her mother's old yellowed magazine clippings, including one that recited that little ditty about the Soong Sisters of China.

> *One loved money,*
> *the other loved power,*
> *and the third loved China.*

She knew that May Lynn was right. Disguise is everything. Only she wished she knew for sure whether it was a disguise of power or a disguise of powerlessness.

"When did I ever say anything that could even be remotely interpreted like that?" disputed May Lynn. But she noticed Sue Mei's disquiet and offered, "We'll go shopping at Sandra's of Vancouver. Nothing but the best will do for my honey."

However, when they got there, they found a health-food store instead. It was another low blow, and Sue Mei seemed to crumple a little more. Just when and where did we get old, she wondered, watching May Lynn wander up and down the plank aisles in sturdy leather walking shoes, looking at vitamins and avocados. Her hair was quite peppery now, but her smile at the clerk in a red gingham apron who handed her a free bag of popcorn was still as fresh as the day they met. Her face was full of fine fret lines though her eyes were amazingly childlike; and she was immensely pleased with herself, searching out Sue Mei to tell her, "That sweet young thing over there informs me that popcorn is a very good source of roughage."

"Well, it constipates the heck out of me," commented Sue Mei rather dryly. Nobody offered her little free samples when she stomped by.

Luckily the little Mozart Tea Shop was still across the street, and they ducked in for tea and cake. But it was crowded, and May Lynn noticed how Sue Mei's face clenched a little more, so she asked ever so sweetly if they could get ahead of the lineup, because her friend was feeling faint. And people, being as kind and generous as she knew them to be, readily agreed.

"Remember when we first met, Meimei? We made a date to meet here for lunch. D'you remember?" May Lynn asked after they were served.

"No, I thought we had lunch in the cafeteria," replied Sue Mei, watching May Lynn circling her upside-down cake with little jabs and pokes.

"This cake is far too rich for me," May Lynn said aside, and Sue Mei knew she would inevitably pass the cake over to her. That was the reason she looked the way she did, and May Lynn looked the way she did.

"Well, yes, we did," May Lynn continued. "The practical side to us took over, as it always does. You only had an hour for lunch. Remember? You were typing in that horrid little – what did you call it? – cesspool at the university. And I had my little Console back in those days. I had it parked in a special hiding place in the bushes, right next to the library, remember? Those were the good old days when one could still play cat and mouse with the authorities. Anyway, I could have gotten you here and back in an hour. So what if you were a few minutes late? It would have given your supervisors a cheap thrill, and something to gossip about for a few days. They were a dreadful lot. I don't know how you stood it there for fifteen years."

"Seventeen years." Sue Mei sniffed. And yes, of course she remembered the day she glanced up from her Smith Corona typewriter and saw a stylish woman singling her out. She was both surprised and embarrassed to find herself being introduced to Miss May Lynn Merriam, a post-doctorate fellow of the University of Texas who brazenly strode up to her desk at the rear of the typing pool and asked if she was Miss Sue Mei Chong, and would she please have lunch with her soon. Say, one day this week?

"I . . . I bring my lunch," Sue Mei had stammered, dumbfounded, as the clacking typewriters around her came to an abrupt and mysterious standstill. May Lynn smiled down at her and made a mockingly loud suggestion that they might have a mutual acquaintance about whom they would need to chat at length.

Sue Mei noticed how tall and slim she was, and how she threw her shoulders back in that way of hers, and how she was not at all chinese until she spoke specifically to Sue Mei. But thereafter she was very much chinese, and not at all intimidated – a young, female, certainly not beautiful but energetic associate professor of asian studies from the United States, where, according to Sue Mei's indignant supervisors, "they have none of our kind of politeness at all."

"Well, I never thought I'd live to see a yellow-eyed chink! Who does she think she is?" Sue Mei heard one of them hiss at the other. And it was true that the colour of her eyes was amazing – the palest green hazel. Since then Sue Mei had always thought of them as golden.

It was a job, and she was lucky to land even that much. Back in those postwar days, they were still very good at the wartime scare tactics. After Beakins gave her the good ol' heave-ho – wait a minute . . . first they told her she was the best heavy-duty tractor mechanic they ever had and then they gave her the boot – it took her years to get over the injustice of it all. Sharing dingy little rooms in chinatown with her ailing mother did nothing to lift her spirits. Trolley cars in the sweltering heat of summer, library books with her boxed lunches, runs on the heels of her Woolworth nylons; it wasn't so much the lack of prospects as the dearth of surprises to which Sue Mei could not submit.

May Lynn was a surprise. In fact, she has been the most fabulous surprise after glittering surprise for twenty-four years now.

"Oh you. You always had to be shown how to enjoy yourself," May Lynn has baited more than once.

"Oh you. Things were different for you. You didn't look chinese. And you had all the advantages," Sue Mei would briskly snap back.

May Lynn sat in the tea shop, looked smug and let her eat cake. Admittedly she did enjoy teasing Sue Mei a bit too much, but that was because she liked to think that she understood her. Sue Mei hadn't changed much in all those years. A face that she wore like a paper bag in public; she would never be able to recreate herself with enough contentment or security or even adequacy. However, her one saving grace was that she clearly preferred herself like this.

And whatever Sue Mei prefers May Lynn prefers to let her be. For instance, ages ago, May Lynn used to drive her home after work, and Sue Mei used to gripe about how expensive an automobile was to operate, so May Lynn bought a brand-new shockingly expensive Town and Country convertible.

"But I can afford it now, because I'm moving to a much cheaper place. Really, the rent is going to be incredibly low." She remembered following Sue Mei into Capital Poultry and Fish at Keefer and Gore as she told her this. Sue Mei wasn't intending to buy; she just wanted to harass the cheating old goat in there by telling him he sold his halibut steaks for a good cent more a pound than the Five Star on Carrall.

"Oh? Where are you moving to?" inquired Sue Mei as she poked at the fanlike gills of the codfish on ice.

"Well, the widow Quan upstairs is going to move in with her youngest daughter's family, so I've put in a deposit for her suite with Mrs. Wong of Sunbeam Realty."

"You actually went to see those crooks? Mrs. Quan upstairs in my building?" asked Sue Mei, her eyes intense and black and tartled, her complexion apparently too brown, nose too flat and too fleshy, her lips sculpted, hair thick in a full-bodied french roll. And as May Lynn nodded yes, she thought Sue Mei was absolutely gorgeous.

"In my building? Are you crazy?"

"Well, yes and no. I mean, think about it! I'll save both time and money, since I drive you home every day. And I won't have to drive back and forth across town to pick you up whenever we go to the movies or something. I thought that would impress you. And it's almost like the penthouse suite, so I won't lose my social standing or anything like that."

"You don't belong in a falling-down chinatown tenement building full of . . . of dumb old women!" yelled Sue Mei, recoiling from the very idea of such a distressing arrangement.

"Well, golly, you don't have to be such a snob about it. An opening like this doesn't come up every day," cried May Lynn to Sue Mei's back because she was already storming out of the fish store.

"Don't you dare!" were Sue Mei's fatally attractive last words on the matter.

"Does this mean . . . I'm still invited to dinner, aren't I?" May Lynn called after her.

"Actually it was her mom who invited me," she explained to the cheapskate at Capital Poultry and Fish, "so I better buy some fish or something."

May Lynn knew Sue Mei well enough to know that she would never leave her mother to move in with her, and her mother would never leave chinatown, so May Lynn had to be the one to learn to live with Sue Mei and her dogge inhibitions.

On June 6, 1962, May Lynn was in the middle of publishing a paper titled "A Reinterpretative Study of the Classics of Mountain and Sea." Sue Mei, who had worked by her side all along, knew as much if not more about the subject. They were reading over the proofs in May Lynn's office when they heard a dull and dense thud downstairs. May Lynn's dog was just a big ol' galloping puppy then, prone to mischief, so May Lynn went downstairs to investigate and was the first to reach Sue Mei's mother, who was laid out in the narrow landing in the hallway. May Lynn gently lifted the old woman's head as her eyes glazed over and her lips turned purplish.

"Yew Sue Mei mama" were her last words, fired off perhaps randomly, perhaps not. Since then, May Lynn had wondered every so often what the old woman had meant to say, but Sue Mei was so devastated by her mother's death that May Lynn just grabbed at their literal meaning. She hadn't even realized this until a few years ago when she began to notice that unfailingly, at the end of supper, Sue Mei served her oolong tea and the gruel made with the fragrant rice stuck on the bottom of the pot, exactly as she had done with her mother. And – wouldn't you guess? – of course May Lynn slurped it all up whether she wanted to or not.

She should have initiated a move immediately after the death, but the years slipped away unnoticed, and Su-lin slipped in unnoticed, and Sue Mei kept having to fix up the place, and so on and so forth. So now that they were being threatened with eviction, May Lynn knew very well that Sue Mei would in fact dig in further and prepare for the fight of their lives.

"May Lynn, I think you may be right." Sue Mei revved up her big motor right there, in the dainty tea shop. "We really shouldn't allow ourselves to get herded along by profit mongers."

May Lynn watched with a wide knowing smile; she couldn't imagine when she had mentioned anything like that, but Sue Mei had a fascinating interpretation of life that was all her own.

"And what about the other tenants – Chou Taitai, the foreigner from China, and Sammy Lee, that bag of bones who never contributes his fair share of work," she ran on.

"And look at old Granny Yen Kwei on the ground floor. What will become of her? She's lived there for fifty-five years, for gosh sakes..."

"And predicting for the past five, with amazing conviction, that she's going to die for sure," added May Lynn, "with the coming of each first harsh frost. However, it is true that she has never had to predict where, since it is an absolute given that it will be at home, where all the memories are. It's all a part of her inalienable rice. Besides, the rent's unbelievably cheap. So what are we waiting for, dear heart? Let's finish our tea and get out there to start up our earth mover."

"We... two old bags? We can't even keep up with this damned crazy world, never mind put a dent in it," said Sue Mei, collecting her gloves and purse.

"Shopping bags," contributed May Lynn in another vein. "We're shopping, so we're two old shopping bags."

"Oh you, you can't take anything seriously." But the important thing was that Sue Mei laughed all the way home.

When Sue Mei set out to find the slum landlord responsible for their eviction, she was surprised to be directed to an address in the old working-class neighbourhood of Kitsilano. There she found herself gawking at the mini-skirted, upbeat colours of the law offices of Ward, Wade & Wong. She had to write down the name of Wong Gum Lung for the pretty, perplexed receptionist.

"Is this how you write Danny's name in chinese?" she asked as she swung off her little office perch and tugged at her skin-tight hot pants. She seems very nice, thought Sue Mei, as she watched the long lime-green nylon legs stride away as the woman took the note in to her boss.

Sue Mei's heart began to thump when she saw her nephew approaching. She wondered if she shouldn't have prepared herself better for this moment, even though deep inside she knew she had been preparing all her life. But even as he approached, and she could see that the man she had feared all her life had become young all over again, she knew that the passing of time had no meaning – never has.

Her nephew, Danny Wong, was the same tall graceful man with confidence in his face and clean lines to his dark conservative suit. He had the very same steadfast blank gaze that she remembered when she was very small and vulnerable, dressed up in a painfully expensive, newly starched dress and pinafore, and she with her mother knelt before her father to humbly beg for a bit, just the tiniest bit of legitimacy. Sue Mei also remembered that her mother did not ever sob except late at night, so she stood up very straight.

He came right up to her, and he was blameless. And he would continue to be a man in the blessed power of his prime, generation after generation, for all eternity. He looked at her, but did not, at first, recognize who she might have been.

"This is my late grandfather's name. You knew him well?" He was smiling affably and reached out his hand casually to her, as his grandfather would have done to his peer. She was flattered and utterly charmed in spite of herself, and, of course, flustered. After all, he seemed to suggest to the dinosaur, times have really quite changed, haven't they? His hand was powdery dry, warm and very masculine.

"Of course," he said, "how do you do, Auntie – ?" Danny referred to the eviction notice, "Auntie Sue Mei. And how is your mother?"

"She's been dead . . ." uttered Sue Mei, completely startled. Then she clamped her mouth shut, embarrassed at having to tell him for how long.

"Oh, I am so sorry. I must have been thinking of someone else. I see you live in one of our buildings in chinatown." He smiled affably again and waved his hand casually in the direction of his private office with its spectacular waterfront view.

"Of course" – as Sue Mei got into the meat of her story to May Lynn and Su-lin, they all sat down to dinner, savouring every detail, from the wonderful aroma of a clear winter-melon-and-pork-bone broth cooked over low heat, delicately flavoured with dried shrimp, to the enticing texture of beef-flank strips stir-fried in garlic and onions and simmered for just a minute in home-canned tomatoes and the steamed rock cod swimming in a picturesque pond of oil, soy and emerald greens, and finally the tightly packed barbecued duck from Kay Wah on the table in front of them – "he was absolutely ruthless, but he didn't reckon on us being so different from what he imagined we would be. I think he supposed that we would be too terrified or ashamed of our lowlife bastardized selves to make a peep, much less to threaten to yell it out loud for all chinatown to hear. But times have really quite changed, haven't they?"

She picked up her chopsticks triumphantly and lightly touched the white fluffy round mound of rice in her bowl. Su-lin, she had noticed, preferred to press her rice down. May Lynn ignored hers altogether, in favour of the savouries.

"Aw, I betcha he knew you right away then." Su-lin launched in, as Sue Mei and May Lynn stuffed big juicy pieces of duck into their mouths. "I mean, you look just like him, don't you know? And of course Danny must know what a philandering old shit his forefather was. Hah, I betcha he's had to deal with this one more than once, eh?"

"Hard to say how many women the old tyrant . . . used like my mother," Sue Mei said, with her mouth awkwardly full.

"Well, I remember that I was shocked when I first laid eyes on you," added Su-lin. "I thought you were one of his real daughters. You looked snotty enough when you came into the Smilin' Buddha, remember, a long time ago. Golly gee whiz, what a dive that place was, but were the tips ever good! All those big burly loggers. Hey, d'ya wanna see where I broke my arm during that big ol' riot? Forty-eight stitches, can you believe it?"

This was one of Su-lin's often repeated gestures, but May Lynn looked at the spot Su-lin pointed to on her arm with the same fresh attention as the first time. Sue Mei smiled to see them friendly again. It helped to have May Lynn's mouth occupied with good food. Su-lin told the same story about how her high heel got caught when she was hurrying to take shelter during a drunken brawl that erupted at her place of work. And she fell against a table full of beer glasses.

However, the tender moment didn't last. May Lynn swallowed hard and challenged Su-lin, "What do you mean 'one of his real daughters'?"

"You know very well what I mean – one of his 'legit' daughters." Su-lin's glare was much deadlier than her verbal jabs.

"Well, then say 'legit,'" demanded May Lynn. "Don't Sue Mei and I look 'real' to you?"

Sue Mei didn't interfere any more, even though she thought May Lynn rode Su-lin unmercifully. After all, Sue Mei had met May Lynn's mother in San Francisco – a dear, sweet, diplomat's wife, long retired with hubby number four who was a sri lankan from London, so she understood that Su-lin and May Lynn would never, ever see eye to eye.

May Lynn's mother had the most amazing mass of flyaway, angelic white hair. She travelled the U.S. extensively, raising "jillions of dollars" for various third-world causes. She still spoke with an enchanting texan drawl and said things like, "Honey, if y'all ever see me getting conservative, do me the supreme favour of delivering a good swift kick to my ass end!"

It was difficult for Sue Mei, who had always thought of herself as a common garden variety of bastard, to imagine this vibrant woman in a clandestine liaison with a chinese man in 1924. Yet apparently May Lynn's mother, as a young audacious student of anthropology from the University of California, thought nothing of turning Wong Golden Dragon, who in his day was a vicious, small-time crook, on his head, or returning home, pregnant with his child. May Lynn grew up as pampered and privileged and unconventional as her mother at her grandparents' cliff-clinging house overlooking the Pacific Ocean on Fanhill Island, just north of San Francisco.

May Lynn's mother proudly asserted that she once spoke three dialects of the chinese language. And she had passed by Vancouver with Henrietta Mertz, the famous anthropologist, who was also a dear old friend of the family, because they were interested in investigating some evidence of an ancient chinese landing on the west coast of North America, way, way before Columbus. And, thank goodness, May Lynn's mother suffered no discombobulation about speaking candidly of her affair with May Lynn's father.

"Well, my dear, that man just about broke my heart to bits. But wasn't I the nincompoop in those days? However, the baby was good. Not just good, she was absolutely perfect."

Yes indeedee, Sue Mei could well appreciate how Su-lin, the middle of seven slave children, a runaway by the time she was fourteen, and one of Wong Gum Lung's common garden variety whores by fifteen, would simply not be able to wrap her small-town redneck sensibilities around that one.

"Now, don't get me wrong. There was not one nasty word

exchanged between Mr. Danny and me." Sue Mei drew them back to her story as a wave of well-being washed over her and her full stomach. "It was all so cold-bloodedly slick and smooth. I had only to mention Su-lin's name to our Mr. Danny once." It was a brilliantly deployed statement, because she knew Su-lin thrived on such mentionables.

Sure enough, Su-lin broke into giggles. "Did you show him my proof?" Su-lin asked.

"Oh no, nothing like that," answered Sue Mei. "He, I'm sure, remembers exactly who you are. No, my basic approach was that we all came from the same seed of the patriarch. And fathers, by their very nature, want all their offspring to thrive, whether we live within his big house or at the weedy edges of his vast lands and estates."

May Lynn chuckled and clapped her hands.

"Then did you tell him to not bother raising the rent for, say, another twenty years?" piped in Su-lin. With the tables turned, there is always the fantasy of power.

"Well, no – not like that. We all know that it's not a good idea to put a man on the defensive. I may have mentioned our re-tired income not keeping up with the current rate of inflation."

"Too subtle," commented May Lynn.

"No," disagreed Su-lin, "it's smarter to keep to the old 'a Wong is never wrong' trick. Sue Mei knows what she's doing." Su-lin threw a long, admiring smile at Sue Mei and reached for her emptied rice bowl, wanting to refill it, but Sue Mei stopped her.

"You eat" she said. "Your rice has gotten cold."

Su-lin obeyed like a child. She often ate last, and she ate as she has always eaten, hunched over her food like a sorrowful lump of a woman-child, shovelling it down her throat in shame. And Sue Mei had always pretended she didn't notice.

She met Su-lin right after her forty-eight very tender stitches on her arm. At the time Su-lin was staying in the manager's apartment above the strip joint she worked in on East Hastings. Sue Mei had bought her a nice box of chocolates and marvelled at how young she must have been when she dared to go against the grain in chinatown and charged Wong Gum Lung with statutory rape.

Su-lin was overwhelmed by the fact that someone, and another woman at that, would be so kind as to pay her a friendly visit, and she did want so much to be friends. At first Sue Mei was just as happy to have tracked down another of Wong Gum Lung's indiscretions, or should she call them soul debts. Because, in the long run, her efforts certainly paid off. But more important, since then Su-lin had become a dear old friend, and the perfect counterpoint to May Lynn and herself. Together they felt as rich and powerful as the Soong sisters of old China.

"When my mother started to go grey at the edges, I knew she was going to die," Su-lin once confessed to Sue Mei. "I promised myself that I was going to bugger off. I was fourteen then. Old enough!

"Oh, I didn't tell any of my sisters. You never knew when they'd turn on you. Mean and unpredictable, we were. We had to be. My sisters would have finked on me for an extra scrap of salt fish.

"Even the littlest ones had to spend days upon days wheel-barrowing cow manure from this farmer's barnyard to our vegetable garden. The poor white kids used to chuck their trash at us.

"I used to think that my old man beat on me the worst because he couldn't stop me from going to school. By the time I was nine, these white biddies came along and threatened him with jail if he didn't let the younger girls go to school.

"Yep, I surely did run away. Left my old man yelling at my mother's corpse, slapping it around – would you believe that?

Well, now when I remember that, I think how horrible. But you know, at the time, I didn't think nothing of it. It was no different from when she was alive, you know what I mean? I guess he was upset that she finally escaped. Jeez, I walked along that pitch-black highway until my feet bled. Got on that CPR ferry at Nanaimo and came right into Vancouver.

"Hah, you know what I found out years later. My sisters weren't so mad that I got away. They were mad because they thought I was selfish not to think of taking any of them with me. But it wasn't like that. At the time I didn't think that I was going to get anywhere, like I had a future or something. I really believed I was going to die. You know how chinese are always saying 'Go die!' "

One day, a few months later, while cleaning, Sue Mei ran across the eviction notices and finally threw them away since nobody had heard a peep from Danny Wong.

"I'll file one, just for the records," said Sue Mei to May Lynn, "but I really don't think they'll come after us again. Do you?"

"No, absolutely not," answered May Lynn. "I think you set them straight this time."

"I betcha they're hoping that we die off soon," said Sue Mei.

"Well, as long as they don't take it upon themselves to help us along," rejoined May Lynn.

"I wouldn't be at all surprised. They are such go-getters these days, aren't they?" Sue Mei joked.

May Lynn smirked as she turned back to whatever she was reading, but Sue Mei wanted to talk.

"I betcha haven't even noticed how I have changed since my little encounter with Mr. Danny Wong, have you?"

May Lynn took off her reading glasses and gave Sue Mei all her attention. Somehow they have never failed to engage each other's interest.

"Right you are there. I guess I have not, so . . . ?" replied May Lynn most companionably.

"Well, for one thing, I am starting to appreciate myself a little. I mean, look at me. I'm fifty-eight years old, with only a bit of a spare tire. I have you and Su-lin, and I don't want for anything. Not a thing. If that doesn't mean that I am content, I don't know what does. And I was thinking how I supported my mom right up until the day she died – in fact, since I was fifteen years old. That's quite something, don't you think? And do you know what else? I have just recently saved the homes of sixteen old ladies who kind of like living with each other, three cranky old men who kind of don't, thirty-three pigeons, five cats, three budgies, two canaries, one very old dog, one cockatiel, ten caged rats and mice and who knows how many loose ones – all in one go!" exclaimed Sue Mei.

"Well, bravo, I say, hear, hear, and absolutely bravo!" exclaimed May Lynn.

"Aannd you know what else? Well, all along, I guess I thought we didn't have much of a life. You know, I felt we – well, not you, but the rest of us – were rejects. In fact, they actually had me believing that I was totally undeserving, and I was supposed to be missing out on even the basics. All my life I felt like that, then felt stupid for feeling like that. You know . . . beating myself up over and over again.

"But the last straw was to have that man that day – our ever so legal regal Danny Wong – come along with all his kind-hearted, new liberal attitudes to tell me that even our shame is worthless and outdated now. Well, after a whole lifetime, I have grown very attached to our leper status, thank you very much. I realized that if that was all we have in this life – so be it! And that slick hotshot, that symbol of everything I was never allowed to be, was even trying to take that away. Can you imagine?" cried Sue Mei fiercely.

"Hear, hear," agreed May Lynn.

"Greedy buggers! They'll reduce you to rubble if you let them."

"Literally." May Lynn looked at Sue Mei adoringly.

"Off with their heads," gloated Sue Mei in all her glory, but then she leaned closer to May Lynn and whispered, "I gotta tell you a secret, though. Actually, I always wanted a son like our Mr. Danny Wong."

"Whatever for?" yelped May Lynn.

"To be legit, I guess," answered Sue Mei patly.

"You've got to be kidding," demanded May Lynn.

"Well, I guess I've gotten over that one too," decided Sue Mei.

"Well, I should hope so," concluded May Lynn, regaining her composure.

DAISY THE
SOJOURNER

. . . the Chinese immigrant coming to this country is denied the rights and privileges extended to others in the way of citizenship; the law compels them to remain aliens.

A. B. Chan, Gold Mountain: The Chinese in the New World

"Is your name really Minou?" I remember I asked the woman with a splotchy red face who was wearing a strange, outdated outfit. But she couldn't hear me over the throbbing blasts of stereo speakers.

"Whadya say?" She leaned over and presented a mushy headful of soft brown flyaway hair close to my mouth. It smelled freshly washed, and I knew there had to be an ear close behind, so I repeated my question.

"Of course not!" she replied. "But you'd better not call me Daisy either. Nothing sends me in a bitch of a rage faster."

"OK! I won't!" I replied quickly. The house party situation that we were both in was unfamiliar to me, as was venturing forth to meet people. But Daisy had looked pretty friendly. Anyway, to make a long story short, she was the first, actually the only, person with whom I struck up a conversation that night.

"How d'ya do." She held out her hand.

Smiling, I instinctively laid my hand inside her clasp, and found it hot and sticky. I stretched my lips even farther, exposing more of my teeth, but all the while thinking of this old wives' saying that a witch will steal a year of your life for every tooth you expose to her. I felt that it was indecent to reveal too many teeth anyway, if only because too much gum showed along with them. No stranger, I was sure, wants to see so much of your leering insides right off the bat.

Daisy didn't need to ask me my name. Instead she started to hum and jiggle to the music. Suddenly, she belched out loud,

"Daisy, Daisy, give me your answer, please!"

I'm half-crazy for you're such a cock-tease!"

And she got the response she was probably after. The women who were dancing cheek-to-cheek feigned shock and snorted indignations at her.

"Minou!" the big-bummed Sylvia deplored. "We couldn't have possibly heard such obscenities from your girlish lips."

Then the bigger-bummed Lorna sashayed past and screeched, "Not one of those confused heterosexuals in here!"

I remember I laughed, not, I hope, because that was the thing to do when one is the frozen new flavour in a cliquey feminist artists' collective, but because I really did feel more relaxed and impetuous. Suddenly I wanted to belong to a madcap fringe of creative lunatics too. Just like them, I felt I could have shamelessly jutted out my derrière and raspberried the whole damn world too, if I had really wanted to.

Funny, it's been eight years since that night I met Minou, and it's been five since I last saw her, face to face, but I still think about her. But until her letter arrived today, I hadn't noticed that I do. It isn't really a letter, more a photocopied bulletin about her life in New Zealand, which she sent to all her friends. It feels funny that it should arrive now – I mean, at this particular time, at my neat and tidy, already paid off home, which I share with my husband, Huey, and where quite frankly I have been slumped in a chair for days like a dead person, feeling sorry for myself. I was again thinking of either leaving him or killing myself.

"Did this letter make you cry?" he asks when he comes home from work.

"No, of course not," I reply. "I just felt like shedding a tear or two – over missed opportunities perhaps . . . for . . . for more meaningful associations with others," I shakily tack on.

"What's for dinner?" he asks.

I guess I could easily resent a question like that, especially at this particular moment, but I don't. I really couldn't care less any more. Besides, I tell myself, it is perfectly safe for me to say anything I like to my husband, if only because he doesn't take anything I say seriously. In fact, I ask him if he remembers Minou, just so that he can mention again that he never understood why I wasted my time on someone like her.

But I remember that party for a couple of reasons. One was the homemade beer, which I had never had before and immediately liked. Another was that I called Minou a slut and cheap, for which I felt incredibly guilty. Of course I blame the beer, which slurred my speech. I had meant to exclaim, "My, but you're slick and chic!" referring to her outfit – some sort of outrageous '67 miniskirt with matching net stockings with a gaping hole on her meaty left thigh. We were both in the kitchen by then, where the music was not as invasive, so, when my words inverted themselves, I was clearly as startled as Minou.

When the time came to go home, I insisted on driving Minou and her sleepy daughter. The little girl, five years old at the time, still clad in a skimpy sleeveless sundress, shivered in the early-morning cold. It was already October, with mist on the windshield. I asked if the kid didn't have a coat or something. Minou mentioned that she did have one somewhere.

"Oh, she'll be fine, and her name's Margaret," she declared. For the rest of the ride home, Minou kept the conversation sprinting. She said that she appreciated my conscientious driving and interpreted it as a protective gesture towards little Margaret.

"Say, your car's not a junker," she said. "That's a change."

Because I have always had this notion that caucasian children are tougher, had more "yang" or something, and fare better in adversity, I readily accepted Minou's child-rearing expertise. As for my driving, I always hunch and peer over my steering wheel because I'm nearsighted. And I drive slowly because I tend to be absentminded, or "stoned on natural endorphins," as my then-fiancé, Huey, would remark. And my brother had just given me the car, being the kind of guy who could beat the shit out of you one moment, then give you the shirt off his back the next. Huey, of course, took over the care and maintenance of it in his parents' garage. He didn't really have to, since my uncle is a mechanic, but of course Huey insisted.

"You can cover her up with my towel. It's the one I use when I go swimming at the aquatic centre," I still felt obliged to offer.

"She's fine. Really. We're almost home." It turned out that they lived two blocks past where Huey and I lived in sin, in our first cramped apartment with a balcony, which faced a newly erected concrete wall.

"Just what do you think you are doing?" It turned out that Huey had waited up for me that night, just so that he could ask me that question in that patient way of his.

Was it so odd to leave one's boyfriend at home to go to an all-women bash? I wondered. He already knew about what he labelled my "about-face." I had had a ghastly falling-out with a certain women's auxiliary in chinatown over some artwork I did for them for nothing, no less. I had become tired of not being appreciated in that community and had decided it was time to detour my social consciousness. So I veered over a few city blocks, from chinatown to Commercial Drive, or "from race to gender," as I saw it.

I described Minou and Margaret to him, and said, "I like her. She's so lighthearted and fun. Imagine just allowing yourself to be swept by the wind into some strange city where you don't even know a soul. Imagine being that reckless and vibrant and wild."

"Only because she's a *lofan*," Huey snarled into his flat, square pillow. "What would you think of her if she were chinese and like that? I bet you wouldn't give her the time of day."

The next day, and certainly not out of spite, I met Minou and Margaret again. Either I was being true to my traditional upbringing, or Minou just had a quick and easy gift of gab, because as we walked we got right into her family history.

After a fleeting love affair during the war, Minou's mother became a valiant young single mother living on welfare in Quebec. Minou told me of one desolate Christmas when her mother had emptied bottles of cheap vino and filled them with her own chagrined tears, because they had received a Salvation Army food hamper. Her mother's flimsy cover had been blown; her neighbours saw them as poor. As the child, Minou thought the hamper was wonderful, as were all gifts, but years later, as a struggling single mother herself, Minou also viewed welfare offices and her appointments with them as totally humiliating experiences, unbearable without a crutch.

And on that day, that crutch turned out to be me.

"You don't look as though you need their stinking welfare money," Minou told me when she asked me to go with her to the Ministry of Health and Welfare H.Q.

I was on UIC at the time, but I was intrigued by that certain look that Minou thought I had. I spent twenty minutes or so in a shiny fluorescent office, sitting in a vinyl orange chair, with some pleasant-looking staff people and client people, glancing out the window at our west coast, indian summer scenery, and marvelling at this happy-go-lucky way of being poor. Minou's welfare officer was a chatty Kitsilano-progressive type in brown tights and burgundy chinese cloth shoes. I'll bet she didn't even know I was with Minou. Afterward, to recover from the ordeal, we hopped into my car and headed off for italian gelatti and cappuccino. Minou wanted to treat, but I wouldn't have it.

After that, we did a lot of things together – M&M and I. She told me that she invests a lot of energy in her friends. When I discussed her choice of words with Huey, he dourly pointed out that it was as if I was listening to a poor-quality recording, but instead of investigating the reasons for the scratches and failing sounds, I was the type to get sucked in to pressing my ear closer and turning up the volume. That was his scenario, and, boy, it sure didn't have to gibe with mine.

I loved Minou's wayward fervour for every project and person she took on. One new friend was a waitress in a steakhouse who lived in a one-bedroom apartment in a brand-new high rise in the west end. She invited M&M to stay overnight, thrilling them with the heated swimming pool and the nightlife and the sharp contrast to their living arrangements in the second storey of a rickety old house, where they shared a bathroom in the hall with the third-floor tenant, a creepy quiet guy who worked seasonably as a logger. Minou resented cleaning the toilet after him, and counted the days until he'd "disappear in some bush for good."

I, on the other hand, was curious to know why Minou disliked him when he didn't seem that different from her men friends, most of whom were laid-back seasonal flunkies who wore flannel shirts and talked a lot about being "workers." I quickly learned in french, that if one is going to wear flannel shirts, one had better do it with flair. And if one is to be a seasonal flunky (the actual name for those employed in logging camps as kitchen helpers), then one had better do it with a defiant glint in one's eye. And one had better have been to Europe too. Minou pooh-poohed me for being such a provincial dope, and I shuddered at the fragile difference between being perceived as determinedly laid-back with options and being merely inadequate without options.

I met Lois, the steakhouse hash-slinging waitress, too. We were repulsed by each other the minute we met. I don't know why. Perhaps it was because she was young and shaky, pale and insipid. I could tell that she, like me, was taken by Minou's vibrant charm. Then Minou told me that Lois was a former mental patient. I don't know why I wasn't surprised to hear that, just as I wasn't surprised to learn that Minou had had to break ties with her. Apparently Lois went bonkers one day and started shouting hideous obscenities at M&M. I asked Minou if she was certain that Lois didn't have a reason for her outburst. And Minou replied, "Not a even coherent one, never mind a valid one."

I had by then entered nursing school and read enough nursing texts to put Lois's impressive behaviour down to "poor impulse control." I'm sure that helped Minou feel vindicated.

I put away Minou's letter, which contains infuriatingly general news about her new environment in New Zealand, the social scene, the weird accent and Margaret's difficulties at school. The guy she had followed over there is long gone, but she has found something much more buoyant – a job. There is no indication she plans to come back. Huey and I are obviously has-beens for her. So there. I have no choice but to follow Huey around our well-insulated home, with vague complaints about a hollow feeling I get in the pit of my stomach.

As Huey and I sit down to dinner, something occurs to me. I realize that many of the arguments that Huey and I had about Minou were really about how foreign she felt to us.

"Huey," I say, "I think I know why people are so prejudiced. They react to everything according to how familiar or foreign it is to them. Think about it, Huey, it's your family that signals — in fact, decrees — your response to everything you will do in your entire life. Chinese family values are a double whammy, don't you think? Really, there's no point to reaching out these days. People are so predictable." I don't know why, but my voice cracks under unidentified pressure.

Out of the blue, Huey says, "You know, you should have stuck to nursing. If this is what you learn in those women's studies courses you take, or whatever you think you're doing these days, then, yeah, what is the point?"

I laugh lightheartedly, then I get up, go to the kitchen and start to frantically chop onions for our dinner tomorrow. All the while I blubber about the familiarity of onions and their irritatingly predictable way of tearing up my limited vision. Huey looks hurt. After a while, he puts on his jacket and goes back to his mother's. It's so hard to escape one's present tense, I think; much easier to stick one's nose into someone else's past.

Back when we were at our friendliest (or should I say most familiar?), Minou told me that before I happened along, she had just broken up a short, intense friendship with a woman in the collective named Marilyn. Marilyn was another mystery to me — not so much because she was a lesbian, but because she never gave me one iota of her attention. She made me feel my lack. I used to have to look the other way when she and her intimates gazed longingly, intriguingly, achingly across the room at each other. Well, apparently, along came Minou, the fascinated groupie, also an accomplished little flirt, who led Marilyn on a bit too far, which she lived to regret. Within the collective there were claims that the straight women felt oppressed by gays, and gay women by straights – strong, cackling currents and crosscurrents snapping back.

"But you and your boyfriend are allowed to fall in love, and you don't have to be token anything for anybody," Minou remarked at a time when Huey and I were still newly in love and easy with love.

"Huh?" Being tested woke me up (though being token was all too familiar). "I guess," I answered groggily.

Huey's most romantic thought was that we were like honey and bee. And he wanted us to do everything together. Take the garbage out together. Change the oil in the car together. Go to nursing school together. A chinese girl holding hands with a chinese boy seemed respectable enough for public viewing; in fact it was encouraged. Since I had not yet heard of patriarchal privilege, I was not aware that marriage and the rituals thereof and thereby were one massive setup. I didn't learn that until it was too late for me.

Minou enjoyed seeing me with my familiar, who always grinned boyishly and charmingly to her face. I have often wondered when exactly she decided that chinese men were the cat's meow. It was really quite comical. While Minou admired my tangled turtledove love nest, I was fascinated by her unfettered ability to roam about that big unknown out there. I always dreamed of escape and adventure but lived quite predictably, driving carloads of family and relatives to and from chinatown. The displaced person's instinct for durability and the survivor's fear of annihilation were definitely the heritage that our disenfranchised Gold Mountain-sojourning forefathers dump-trucked on me, and I married into more carloads of family and relatives, thus binding my feet.

It was my dad who always hackneyed caucasians to death, usually for their perverse egos, their philandering, wanderlust ways, their rampant disharmony with the universe and so on and so forth. In other words, if I married one, or lived in sin as they were always doing, then I'd die horribly alone like one. I always nodded agreeably at him until I nodded asleep.

Yet my dad liked Minou. I was driving him to chinatown because yet another old uncle in our clan association had just died when I spotted M&M on the street and picked them up. Dad was so busy lecturing me on the ol' chinese-stick-together theme that he didn't have time to ask what this woman's husband did. He just remarked that she had a friendly face, and was older than me. He liked me to associate with older people.

I remember the day Minou dropped in on us after supper with her newfound friend, a chinese guy named Eddy. She looked radiant, but Eddy alerted me as soon as he followed her through the door. When he realized that Huey and I were also chinese, he stiffened. She gave me her usual full-bodied french-canadian kiss; and he hugged the wall.

Eddy guarded the tea that we served him, but I made a point of prying some dilute information out of him. He said he was a medical student from Toronto in town for an academic conference. Originally sent from Hong Kong, he had been in Canada for five years, studying. He hadn't done much of anything except study, but now, all of a sudden, he wanted to learn to ski.

As Minou and he got up to leave for the slopes, I automatically said, "Have fun," but I realized that was redundant for Minou. I should have said something like, Look before you leap! But that would have been redundant of me.

M&M were in seventh heaven for many months. Eddy winged across the country whenever he could. Minou started conversational mandarin lessons. She became an expert on cantonese restaurants in Vancouver, the hong kong bourgeoisie, and lightly steamed rock cod.

During this period, she dropped in on Huey and me a lot. I think she wanted to ask me that all-important question, but we both knew that feminist collective decorum does not allow such wavering, no matter how human the frailty. Still, Minou had many ways of hinting at it, so finally I gave my blessing: "Yes, sweetie, I think you'll make a great doctor's wife."

There were a couple of snags, though. The first was that the shithead was already married to a sweet shy wife who barely spoke english and worked as a chambermaid to support them both. The second was that Eddy never actually made it into medical school. He was in dentistry. Minou and Eddy's wife wept bitterly, long distance, when they finally zeroed in on what had happened.

Poor Minou. Of course I had no sympathies for that creep Eddy, but I suppose I could imagine his predicament. I know all about those stupid chinese rules on high achievement. His parents, who probably weren't that well off, had barely scraped enough together to guilt-trip Eddy over here for a good gold-mine education. And he did his filial best, but the poor idiot never knew what came over him when he was far from the beaten path and Minou with her mushy soft hair fixed her lovely grey eyes on him and almost thought out loud that chinese men are this kitty cat's meow.

I don't know why it was so hard for me to accept the changes in Minou's attitude on life. I could hardly expect her to be as happy and carefree as before, and though I was disappointed by her defeat, I felt comforted that she was no different from me. The more women with our feet encased in concrete the merrier, I always say.

Not too long after this mishap, Huey, of all people, surprised me when he asked, "Does Minou blame us for what happened, since we're chinese and Eddy's chinese? Maybe she thinks all chinese are like that."

I gave that a good deal more thought, especially since Minou had marched up to me that morning and told me that Margaret had been picking up a lot of racist views at school.

"She learned the word *raghead* from a chinese kid." She'd pounced, then tapped her claws as if waiting for me to explain how my race could be racist towards other races. And don't I wish I knew.

Meanwhile, things changed as they inevitably will. Huey and I finished nursing school. With the help of his parents, we bought a little starter home and moved away. The feminist artist collective folded after twenty years of learning how to survive. Minou found a temporary job teaching english as a second language. And Margaret grew up fast. She was slightly withdrawn, especially when compared with her mother.

I remember a dream I had about M&M. It was late at night, the aftermath of some kind of fiery holocaust. Huey and I were walking anxiously up their street, when little Margaret, nude and frightened, ran up to us. Farther up the hill, Minou was walking rapidly away to meet her friends. We called and tried to catch up with her but couldn't. But Margaret had calmed down and seemed content to hold on to us and suck her thumb. So we took her to the big bingo hall on the corner of our block. There we sifted through piles of other people's clothes to find something to cover her with.

Minou had a dream about me as well. In it, I had a beautiful baby girl. As M&M visited me, I had the kid all sparkling clean, immaculate in a frilly frock. I was tying ribbons all over her, but when I started to wrap her in clear cellophane, Minou cried out that I would suffocate her.

Once when Margaret was about eight years old, and I remember this vividly, she suddenly told me, "Minou isn't a good friend to have, you know."

It was a precise warning, given when her mother was in the

bathroom. Margaret didn't even glance at me when she said it. If I was too slow or too dumb to catch it, then tough luck! As fast as she said that, her face smoothed back to bland, impenetrable innocence. She ignored me when I asked her to repeat what she had just said. I thought I heard wrong, like the difference between "slick and chic" and "slut and cheap." But by then it didn't really matter to me. I knew girls her age tend to put too much emphasis on friendship and all that is familiar.

When can I return to the Mountain of Tang with a full load?
From ancient times, those who venture out usually become worthless.
How many people ever return from battles?

Island: Poetry and History of Chinese Immigrants
on Angel Island 1910–1940, "Poem 34"

SAFE SEX

AT THE TIME I was sure that it would not have happened if I had stayed encapsulated in my own car. I picked it up somewhere between my mom's house and my place. From seats in public transit. At the very least my little car, Teresa Toyota, though gutless and full of holes, is mine. I can lock her up, and I have some control over who plants their secretive flora on her private vinyl insides.

My old man and old lady, eighty-four and seventy-seven, tweedle-dee and tweedle-dum, live in Victoria. They shuffle about in that dilapidated house of theirs, blind and deaf, tripping and falling, dropping boiling water and snapping wrists. It's a pain for me since there's only my sister and I to clean up. And I don't mean that there's just the two of us. There are five brothers as well and plenty of nephews, but they seem, as always, to be exempt from wetting their hands.

I live and work in Vancouver now. So it gets expensive, ferrying my vehicle back and forth between the island and the mainland. Sometimes I get a ride with relatives. But after my mother's second mishap, I finally resorted to investigating public transit. I told myself that I didn't care how I looked to others – like those immigrant men snoring with their unshaven mouths open and their black greasy fingers slipping off their stodgy laps, or, like the little bo peep in the aisle seat, gotten old (and more lost) while looking for those ever elusive rams. And she still wearing the age-old frilly uniform, with edges now frayed.

There's a lot of mental illness out there. I know because I see. And I shudder to think. But it wasn't as if I deserved what I got. I am not in any way an exceptional person. Do I go around looking for trouble? I once asked the mousy, tight-ass, unhappy face in the mirror. No. Neither do I knock myself out. For anything. Uninformed mediocrity, however simple for others, is a kind of studied pastime of mine. It was important for me to party and bridge right through a bachelor's degree, coming out the other end as uninspired as ever.

I'm normal, I tell you. I have my parking space at work. There, the boys chase the girls at office parties. By boys, I mean the engineers and designers. But don't ask me what 'the girls' means. I'm the wrong person to ask. I work for a trendy engineering firm part-time and study art part-time. My apartment is pc, the upstairs of a big house in a desirable location off Arbutus. I try not to keep it too neat and clean, just in case somebody noteworthy drops by. Even though that has never happened in the five years that I have been there.

My landlady has always claimed that she trusts me completely because I am, in her words, "a loner." She leaves me the keys and, of course, the mops to her place when she flies off to Hawaii with her mother three times a year, and brings me cookies, pies, nut loaves and cakes made with all-purpose flour, even though I am allergic to it all. I load them, frozen, into my duffel bag, which I then lug to Victoria to feed to my big strapping nephews.

I think I like myself well enough. I am into neither smashing the state nor upholding the status quo. I repeat, I am not insane or radical or feminist or anything like that. So why me?

As I tried to tell my old friend, Amy Ng . . . no, maybe I know better than to tell Amy. My so-called friends keep telling me that I'm not using my full potential. Who needs them, especially the ones who broke up all the varsity fun to get married? Even worse, married, mortgaged and motherfucked. Excuse me, but doesn't that equate to S-L-A-V-E-S? They've been sneaking up on me at weddings, house warmings and babies' full-month parties to exclaim, "Naomi! You look wonderful. How come short people never get old? Whatcha been up to these days?"

We were once a tight catty circle of friends. Actually I was genuinely pleased to bump into ol' Amy, and truly, I opened right up.

"Oh hi, Amy. Say, that's a nice nose job."

"Oh, you backward little twerp, you," she said. "You're supposed to notice the tan. And then the socially appropriate thing to do is to ask me where and how much? Like that, you savvy fair?"

"How much did the nose job hurt?" I asked.

"Oh, you're a moron's shit," she shot back with a wide smile on her face.

I was totally charmed. I should mention that I was feeling a bit nervous, in fact overwrought, and I was sure it showed. Amy was immediately fascinated by my agitation and excitement. She and I used to belong to a huge sisterhood, which kept us – at least me – vastly entertained during our undergraduate days at UBC. And the fact that we all looked alike had nothing to do with anything. Our lives may have seemed like clichés on the surface, but we really did love each other dearly. Our biggest delight was to get together and shock each other silly. Boo. Eek. Boo. Eek.

"Amy," I began, "do you believe in the supernatural?" I then explained how I was recently on an evening ferry, *Queen of*

Tsawwassen, chugging through the channels, gazing out at the cyanotic waters and mists, when I felt it for the first time. Something touched my hair. I felt it, a firm sweep of a hand or something. I looked all around. It wasn't a very crowded boat. There wasn't anyone sitting nearby. But I'm sure something like that has happened to everyone, hasn't it? Sure it has. And it's usually not a problem, right? One just concludes that some brain waves got crossed, and that's the end of that, right? Except it didn't end there for me.

"What do you mean it didn't end there?" Amy asked. She, still approving my story thus far, dragged me out the patio doors, dumped me into a wet lawn chair and lit up a cigarette. It was too chilly for me, and I shivered.

"Well, I got more of these strange feelings, like I wasn't alone, you know. Like palpable temperature changes. Like prickling on the back of my neck. Like someone was watching me."

"So what? I get that all the time." Amy had to pooh-pooh my story. Unspoken rules. She knew I would have to redouble my efforts to impress her.

"But do the chairs nearby shudder under some kind of weight? Does something breathe on your neck? And something touch your arm?"

"All at the same time?" she asked and flicked her cigarette ash.

"Yes," I replied wholeheartedly, glad that she was getting the picture. "I hopped up like a fool and looked high and low. In the aisles, behind me, all around me. I was positive that someone I knew had seen me and was playing a trick on me. But there was nothing. What few people there were in the upper-deck lounge with me never even noticed. Some lady knitting. A newspaper held up. I was a little freaked, and I went to sit back down, but – and this is no lie, OK? – I sat on someone's lap. Honest to god. An invisible but very solid thigh."

Amy started to pull at the ends of her Suki hairdo.

"Yeah, well, I freaked. I whooped out loud and sprang off that chair so fast. I actually landed in the seat in front of me. Needless to say, everyone was looking at me by then. I standing there, gulping air. Pop-eyed. I think I really alarmed people. But I wasn't going to stick around to find out. I felt so addled and embarrassed I half-ran, half-stumbled to the ladies' room. And there I stayed for a very long time, locked in a toilet.

"Nobody came. Nobody followed. And no way was I going out, you know what I mean? But after a while, of course, I started to feel silly. I mean, who wouldn't? Ultimately I had to arrive at the absolutely necessary conclusion that I had not experienced any of it. Absolutely. None of it. So there. I sneaked a peek.

"Right away, I knew 'it' was still out there. There, in the public washroom that looked normal and was brightly lit, with wall-to-wall mirrors. I don't know quite how to explain how I knew. It was like I sensed the air stir. I didn't exactly see it or hear it, but yet I did, you know."

Oops. Well, what do you know? The story got ahead of me. I remembered to check in with Amy. Too late. She was staring at me with perfectly dramatized horror, but then she narrowed her eyes. Uh-oh.

"Yeah? Well? Then what happened?" she asked with extreme attention. To personal safety.

"Well, I guess I've been on the run ever since," I replied, con and trite, with a big perky smile. But I never lie. Hey, like I've never steered a conversation before. I mean, how many steering committees have I sat on in my time? And I know they have always secretly admired and pitied me for being an Arts 1 major.

"Huh?" said Amy, who did Dentistry.

"Just kidding you. To see if you would believe me."

"Oh, you nut!" She, all friendly and quite relieved, slapped my hand.

"You see, Aim, this is my way of telling you how stressed out I am. All work and no play. I need some sympathy." Yet I knew I was going to get advice.

"Girl, you need to loosen up a bit. Get out more. Give those restless hormones a good workout, you know what I mean? You going out with anyone these days?"

See how tables turn? How I get put on the lam? So I put on the dumb-blonde wig to say, "I go out all the time."

"I mean, is there a special guy?"

Gee, I thought, as usual I don't get it. What's a guy got to do with my hormones? So I asked, "Gee, I don't get it. What's a guy got to do with *my* hormones?"

Before I knew it, it was time to go in.

"And join the others," enjoined Amy. So this is the rest of the story that Amy should have heard, but obviously did not.

I know I'm not crazy. Well, I wasn't crazy back then either. I made myself come out of the john, ramrod stiff, and then I went straight to the most populated part of the ship, the dining room, and sat with my back to the wall, close to the captain's table. All of a sudden, my paperback novel became the most all-consuming purpose in my entire life.

I completely disallowed the feeling that something tickled my neck, the soft rustling on the seat beside me and more of those – somehow they felt reverent – strokes on my hair. I finally tied the freshly washed black mass into a tight knot and pulled my toque down over my ears. For extra effect, I put on my coat and gloves and scowled mightily. I must admit, though, that I do have nice, attractive hair. I like it thick and straight and long. And I love the sweep of its blackness against the small of my back. But no way was I going to let this thing get to my hair. Or me. Or my sanity.

After the boat docked, I sprinted off along the mile-long corridor as fast as my hooves could carry me and my baggage, weaving precariously in and out of the tight herd of foot passengers. My glasses bobbed up and down on my flat perspiring nose; I saw mind-boggling, earth-quaking scenery wildly slashed, but I did not stop and I left the terminal quite breathless and giddy.

First one on the city bus by far, I dove in and hid in the back seats. Gasping and choking, I folded myself tightly over my bag and lay on my side, hardly daring to take a breath. Then I heard footsteps approaching. They stopped in the aisle beside me, but I could not bring myself to look up. Then I realized the lights and engine were not on.

"Hey? Are you all right?" asked a young man claiming to be the bus driver. This was his rest stop, and he was about to close up his bus so he could go for his coffee when I bounded in. He told me I was supposed to get off and wait outside.

"No, please, let me stay in here!" My voice was an unappealing hiss under incredible pressure. Then I remembered that I'd forgotten to pay my fare. I shoved a fistful of change at him. He seemed like a kind, tolerant sort, and being a bus driver, he knew about how women get stalked, so he let me stay. For a minute, I felt so embarrassingly appreciative that I almost kissed his hand. And I have never felt like that, believe me – I'm usually so jaded and pugnacious.

On the long ride home, I kept up my guard, knees strained, stomach hardened, eyes stubbornly cross-eyed with fatigue. Three crowded buses. Thinking how I could have done this smarter, if only I had brought my car, Teresa. A girl needs protection from this hostile planet on the brink. In my vehicle with the windows shut and the doors locked, there would not be a creep in the world who could have touched an enarmoured hair on my head. I imagined my headlights bright, leaving the bowels of the boat, bouncing off the ramps and roadsides, lighting my speedy way back home through the haunting wintry darkness.

By the time I tiptoed home, I thought I was alone, that I had lost whatever it was, until I got a good-night peck on my right cheek. It was a kiss. An innocent, indeed solicitous, kiss at the door of my apartment. Suddenly I no longer cared. I let myself in and collapsed in my tiny enclave in front of my full-length mirror. I stared crazily at myself as if I had never seen the young-gotten-old woman on the floor before. My head mushroom-capped by offwhite knitted wool. My rigid black coat tightly buttoned all the way up, with its oppressive length down to my slush boots. I did not recognize myself; I was terrified of my own netherworld appearance. Who can say for sure what is real, and what is not? Normally I would have put things away in order, but this time I just didn't have the heart and I fell into bed exactly like that.

For the next two days I didn't leave my apartment at all, so I had plenty of time to get a grip on myself. I told myself again that I was not crazy and I could not allow myself to be victimized by these illogical feelings. On the third day I made a point of cheerfully going down to pick up my mail in the front alcove, dressed in my rattiest old housecoat, but as soon as I felt its lovesick presence again, I immediately lost my nerve. I receded up the stairs and squished myself back through the gap of my door like excess toothpaste. And then I went straight to bed for another two days.

By then the office had sent me a rather inquisitive get-well card and an expensive bouquet of flowers. You know how sympathy can actually make a person feel worse? Well, this felt like a kiss of death. I knew I would get canned if it kept up.

For some strange reason, it did not come uninvited into my apartment, but that was hardly reassuring. Obviously, something had gotten into my head and completely taken over. I lost interest in the things that used to preoccupy me, like racketball, and pitch and putt. Instead I sagged and slumped on my sofa and stared for hours. I felt unseen forces were making me rethink the entire meaning of my life. This persecution made me angry. And then my anger totally exhausted me. It felt so unfair. At first I rampaged through my house, then I had a fight on the phone with my boss and quit my stupid job, only to agonize even more and whip myself senseless.

Next, I lost interest in the basics like eating to stay alive, washing to uplift my spirits or even answering the phone to remind me that I was still human. I had slipped off the edge, into an unfathomable nightmare. Who knows how much I would have shrunk from reality if I hadn't been jolted back to life. By a startling dream.

I was very young on a feast day, conscientiously examining the intricacies of a white cooked chicken. I had watched my mother very gingerly submerge the pink of it into a big pot of boiling water, holding back the head with her brass ladle. So I noticed the changes immediately afterward, the disappointing colour, the boiled-stiff tongue poised in a silent squawk, and the dripping, dark, mysterious grotto under the perky bum tail, which I gazed into. My mother, young again, had dutifully placed the platter of sacrificed bird on a specially laid-out table in the front room of our little home. So I, with calm child's eyes, examined every inch of that table, because she told me that ancestors were sitting there on the three chairs she had carefully arranged for them, and they were visiting us. And I understood; I accepted their hushed presence at our solemn little altar, replete with homemade offerings and special meanings, even as it came time for me to go to elementary school.

There the teacher gushed at me in my prettily embroidered gold-brocade coat that had come to me from a faraway grandmother, in a huge boxful of delicious smells, with jade bracelets and gold rings that popped out of the bags of dried mushrooms and chrysanthemum tea. The teacher put me in front of the class, where I tried to explain all these holiday miracles to some boys who snickered until the whole class giggled, and even the teacher, with a tiny silver cross pinned to her lapel, laughed out loud.

The enchantment of being small and childlike again took me by surprise. The revelation bubbled forth, burst through my hard, brittle surface and left me aching and exposed for days. In bed I cried and cried until finally one day I threw my door wide open and felt a slight breeze kiss my face.

People noticed the change in me right away. They came and hugged me, gently patted my hand. I made up with my boss, and I even got my job back with a few improvements. One guy asked me if I was on medication. This surprised me a bit. I just said no, without a wisecrack to follow, and he wouldn't believe me, but I knew better than to try to explain myself.

I have simply decided that this is my story of enchantment. Which is not the same as a fairy tale. In fairy tales, the heroine lives happily ever after, after being released from her enchantment, but I don't believe that. I think the poor sap spends her life trying to get back. But when she does – and in my story, I do – then she finds happiness, I find true intimacy. And erotic satisfaction all on my own.

It's not like me to brag, but it's no wonder that I strut a bit. OK, like today, at London Drugs, I found myself browsing through sales bins full of paperback romances, just because they were all so shiny and new and nice to touch. I am able to see their loveliness now, whereas before I wouldn't have noticed. I didn't have to buy or read any. I just appreciated them for being there, in that bargain basement for those ordinary everyday romantics who riffle through life and wipe chocolate mundanes off their children's faces.

It's like on the street, I see many a poor bugger slogging through the bullshit the way I used to do. Feeling filthy and hungry and lowdown and mean. They hate their lives because they think they're so terribly alone. Or they hate their lives because they're afraid of being hideously alone. But I now know that we are not alone.

Sissy. I've taken to calling her Sissy. Of course, I know it's just a silly name – kind of like that story I told Amy Ng – but it was something to get me over my initial period of adjustment. You know the nervousness of those first crazy moments of naked love?

I felt that she would have to be a woman because I am a woman, but the implications of falling in love with myself temporarily stalled me, when actually all I wanted to do was touch and let myself be touched. By endless metaphor, I mean.

OK, OK, maybe gender was something I made up. Maybe all there is, is gentleness and understanding as I get to know myself. And maybe I have come a long way in my ability to feel my own compassionate caresses, but maybe not far enough, because I still get stumped, like here I am still trying to explain and slot Sissy into a language that will surely discard my meaning.

Since that morning I let Sissy in, my life has been full of marvel. I see details larger than life. I was led to the window overlooking the blustery sky and the bruised waters of English Bay. I had never felt so intensely before. Standing there, I pressed against the biting cold glass. Pelting rain outside, the inside misted by my own breath. I saw myself walking along the seawall, in the drenching sea spray, pressing against the cold wind and downpour, crazy happy smiling. My nose, cheeks and ears were swollen, raw and rosy from countless nips of small sharp teeth. And I was an absolute sponge. The soppiest, most ecstatic sponge ever for all sorts of possibilities.

And then I really was walking on the seawall. And it was a sunny, windy day. And there, on the horizon, appeared someone who was tall and thin, wearing work jeans and a baseball cap. The person required careful examination in order to determine the gender, which was, by the way, androgyny. I saw razor-sharp eyes, a mouth set hard as if against an unspeakable history of betrayal, and hanging from it, that everlasting token of slow burnout – the cigarette.

Sissy and I both agreed that the woman was shaped beautifully, with a womanly sway to all her curves. Although her movements were interestingly outlawed by her six-gun bad attitude, she had considerable allure as a renegade. And I saw how she had to puff herself up in order to create the illusion of more protective bulk. But I could imagine that if she – let's call her Betty – mustered a smile, it would be irresistible.

Just for fun, let's say that I smile at her, and she smiles back, so I ask if she wants to get together for dinner. Say, there is probably nothing she likes better than sumptuous food and intoxicating drink. And indolent hot tubs, where, in my fantasy, we will somehow find ourselves afterward, swirling drunk, giggling on high, out on the limb again.

Can't you picture us together? Betty's kind of nudity will be in spite of herself sensitive and creamy white and as soft as warm butter. But my body will glow as if sunned in the tropics. It will flow over with marvellous substance. Though wet and unclothed, I will not be naked. I will empower myself with the other woman's presence. I am patient and sweet; I can wait to make the first tentative move. And she will gasp at the first touch, as I reach deep into another woman's core of being.

And this may all be a far-fetched illusion, but so are most

love stories. And if that is the case, then nobody needs to be disdainful of it. Just another commuter with a twisted sense of humour, bored to distraction, or should I say distortion, with public transit. I mean, just because I am cradled by unseen support, and the power of love behind our never-ending love stories, this does not mean anybody else has to be led astray.

NANCY DREW
MYSTERIES

THE PORNOGRAPHIC

SHE HADN'T REALIZED how forlorn the situation had become. "Dental dams?" she asked. "What are those?"

When she got her answer, Nancy put her white sox and stiletto heels back on her swollen feet and drove home. After rain, the road was slick and treacherous. Tonight, the night wet. The air? The air restless.

She wondered how she had come to be in a strange woman's place in the first place. After her doctor's appointment, Nancy had felt cut adrift, so she went where the wind blew her. Straight into a women's bar. She had looked out of place, but she got picked up right away. Actually, Nancy had to admire the dyke's guts for picking her up to begin with – her name was Barb, apparently – even though Barbapparent may have just needed a ride home. The first thing she said to Nancy was that she was in the wrong bar. There was no such thing as the wrong bar, thought Nancy, not for someone in her precarious situation and her fuck-me shoes.

In the soft vinyl warmth of her new car, Nancy felt ripe. Her legs and arms were runners, her body the fruit. Ripe, her bodily response, ripe for change, ripe for rebirth. Her baby ripe for birth. A spewing forth of a newly illuminated soul, reincarnated, a little soulful, a little handful, a little powerful. The doctor said that her baby was too small for dates.

"Are you eating well?" the nice doctor asked the high-risk obstetrical problem in a voice as carefully cropped as a suburban lawn.

"Am I eating well?" Nancy pondered the question, blowing it all out of proportion, reeling it out of context. Of course the good doctor didn't notice, nor did she notice how she proscribed with her little prescription pad.

"Nancy, I'm going to send you to the nutritionist at the Eastside Women's Clinic. She's there on Thursdays," the doctor said, seeming to want to help Nancy's kind, intrigued yet repulsed by the possibility of getting too close.

THE EROTIC

At home, Nancy stood on a low stool to get a full view of her self, her body, her sex in the mirror.

If they gotcha by the balls, they gotcha all, she thought to herself. Too bad that didn't rhyme better. Who are they?

"They, you know, they," Nancy spoke out loud, suddenly annoyed at her own denseness, "those that are on the outside."

Who dares venture out these days? So who said that? She watched her mirrored hand slide over the belly, rubbing firmly, full palmed, reassuring. From the outside she didn't realize the sensation of it; from the inside the little creature squirmed with delight.

Barb had been an encounter – any kind of encounter would have done. Barb, the dark, toxic and splintered. Barb, the dialogue fast and dirty, in a language Nancy was fluent in. Barb turned out the more awkward, because she was the more grasping. Nancy smiled to herself; she felt a little superior.

There was an unbearable heaviness that made Nancy reach down. And she was not what she seemed either. She had just swallowed a beach ball, that's all. The heaviness began to ache. She crouched forward, spread her skinny thighs apart, froglike. Her hand fished up her crotch. In the mirror, a long shoulder thrown loose, a slim hand crept into the bush at the base of the dark golden egg. Then bright red blood polishing her toenails, splattering on the bathroom floor. A gelatinous glob gushed out onto her hand. She stared at this incredulously, because in spite of things, Nancy had always been sheltered by the spirit of women.

With the blood, Nancy drew mysteries all over her protruding belly, turning it into a red egg, the same red egg dyed by women to celebrate's a baby's first full lunar month. The smeared skin tightened under the drying blood. The iron, cunt-like smell made her think of animal, made her crouch again, reaching in for more paint, but another hand, this one long suffering, bodyless, stopped her with the gentlest of touch.

No, don't do this, said a voice inside. Go get help. Nancy straightened obediently, but she could not make herself feel a sense of emergency. With a slight turn, she admired her handi-work, noting the long tendrils of red trickling down the entire length of her legs. A luscious floating flower. You know how flowers love to show off their magnificent reproductive organs. Yes, the mirror image was still beautiful. Glassed in but it was still good currency. A slim, adolescent body with a medium-large egglike pregnancy. High-set budlike buttocks, tapered thighs. Thick black hair, fine and wavy. Porcelain-white skin, with a deep-blue-sea aura.

"Look, Mommy, it glows," she said out loud.

Yes, my darling, I see. Nancy has long since learned to soothe herself. Deep, dark disturbance below, a mere ripple on the surface.

"My money's just as good as anybody's," declared the china doll, who then began to float slowly back down to earth.

THEN THE EROTICALLY PORNOGRAPHIC

When her mother died, she became a ward of the Children's Aid Society. Since she was sixteen at the time, they offered her two choices: a foster home if she wanted to prolong her education, or a small bachelor's apartment if she agreed to get a job right after high school. Of course she chose the apartment.

Secretly Nancy had intended to go to university all along. She wasn't going to be a waitress all her life; she was going to become a teacher. Until that summer, when she met that man. What was his name? Grafton? Cornell? Crofton? Black guy, caught in that "yeah, but he's a helluva nice guy" syndrome. Business suit. Class. Older. Managerial. Sitting at one of her tables. Sincere, smiling, intelligent eyes glanced at her name tag.

"Nancy. Nancy, you're very beautiful, did you know that?"

His eyes saw. He saw her stiffen and narrow her eyes in a pained way that told him she didn't.

Forcing an agreeable smile to her lips, she sang out, "Why, thank you, sir. Nice of you to say." Poised to serve with processed humility. "Sir, are you ready to order now?" Her eyes deliberate dots, fill-in-the-blanks eyes.

He approved. He said, "You going places, Nancy?"

Her reply. Her voice clinked like ice. Like cocktail waitresses are a determined breed, or something. Fishing for compliments; nosing for tips. Beggars on the brink, never wanting the men, only their money.

So how did she end up going with him? She liked his black face. He offered to take her. It was business and they both knew it would not last.

So at the very least he got her that summer job at that fancy fertility resort for rich white fuzzy boys and ripe peachy girls. Their anxious face-sucking and groping in the dark made romantic for them with strings of brightly coloured patio lights. Their garden hedged in by primroses; Nancy met Gina hiding out in the weeds. Both of them were spying from the fringes, hooting and tooting, making obscene noises, getting chased, almost caught. Meagre entertainment after the long hours of shit work.

Gina was an italian-french-canadian from Montreal. She was a waitress too. Later on, though, she began to double up as a whip mistress for those slow-to-rise boys. That was when she got mean.

One day they were hiking high in the mountains with the threat of grizzly bears lurking everywhere. Gina and she sprawled out in a meadow, their shirts off, happy as larks, their dark, oiled skin softened by the heat of the sun, breasts draped and pliant, mouths watering, hearts too swollen with passion, life, ambition.

Next thing you know, there was Gina begging Nancy to play along too. Come on, she said, they could make enough money in one summer to last them all winter. Down payment on a van, and Mexico, here they come! Sound good? But Nancy had a better idea. They could go back to Vancouver. They could hang out together. She had to go to school. They wouldn't need much money.

Abruptly Gina turned on her. Forget about the owners hiring you back next summer, she said, unless you take on after-hours clients. For a brief moment in history, Gina betrayed herself and looked almost desperate. The corners of her eyes glistened. Nancy held her back as long as she could, but she pulled away forever.

After that, Gina refused even to look at her, until one day

Nancy deliberately bumped into her and almost upset her tray. Gina whirled around and called her a clumsy chink right in the middle of the dining-room floor. By then the summer season was closing; Nancy was numbed out. She smoked a lot of hashish. And there was this white guy beside her all the time. His name was Gregg. "Drive me back to the city, Gregg," she said.

THEN THE PORNOGRAPHICALLY EROTIC

The bleeding stopped after a while. Nancy lay in worry; she felt the baby squirm against her. Rich as a baby in her womb, she thought, idling between sleep and watchfulness, feeling alone, which in itself isn't bad. In fact Nancy liked being alone, but she was alone in a bleak, lonely world. And that really scared her because sometimes she couldn't tell which was which. Always, this fear creeping, seeping up like cold river water around her trapped body. It took everything she had to not let the panic win, to keep her head up. OK, so it was stupid to go out, she told herself. Maybe the baby has come loose. Stay inside, no matter what, stay very still.

You're safe, Nancy kept reminding herself; the baby's safe. She had a cosy little hiding place all her own now where she could finally be free to be herself. She had locks and chains on her doors, bars on her window, food stockpiled; she had lots of money socked away. If she was very frugal, then she and her baby could stay holed up for a long time. Gregg would surely forget about her. What was she anyway but a petty thief hiding out with mankind's most prized possession – the ownership of women's bodies.

Gregg couldn't possibly know that she was carrying this baby. Even if he did hire some thug to come after her and the pittance she stole from him, she could make herself into one of those invisible, dark-skinned street girls with the sodden bellies and chewed-up faces. She was good at disguises.

But you know that if he finds you, you're dead meat, the brutal voice snuck in. Fuck! she balked. Why do you fucking think like that? That awful panic again, always sneaking up on her. Where did it come from? Why couldn't she just slice it off clean? She ground her teeth and redoubled her efforts to stay very quiet. They would not flush her out; her heart was pounding, her lungs panting, her soul awash with terror.

So she slowed down her breathing, waited out the squeezing pressure in her heart, bargained her way back to safe and warm. She even laughed at herself. Wasn't she good at torturing herself? It is hard work, though – this business of being free.

Nancy went back to playing with her baby and stroking herself. She liked the idea of being a mommy, and giving mother-scented kisses. She had wonderful ways of finding and tickling its precious little butt – when it poked out, she poked in. Oh look! Wasn't she the cutest little thing? Fond memories. Look and see! See Nancy! See Nancy when she was very, very little.

BUT THERE ARE MEMORIES
OF THE EROTIC

She woke up on that old, scratchy fold-down couch of long ago beside a little electric heater, which gave off precious little heat. The air was cold and damp, but she was warm enough under the blankets, and there was nowhere else in the world she would rather be, except snuggled tight as she could against her mom. She got up to look around.

"Nancy, are you cold, baby girl?"

"No, Mommy, I'm not . . . Mommy? Are you still waiting for Daddy?"

No answer. Nancy wanted to look out the window. Maybe Daddy was out there on the street. If she saw a man walking by, she thought it was her daddy. She didn't run to tell Mommy, though. She watched him walk away until it was too dark to see him.

"Nancy, don't squirm so much. You might wake Bobby."

"Mommy, I'm cold," whined her little brother.

"Squeeze in against me tighter, Bobby. Nancy, lie down."

Nancy lay down. She wanted to feel her mother's warm breath on the top of her head.

BUT THERE ARE MEMORIES
OF THE PORNOGRAPHIC

Then she got bigger – big enough for raging. She saw him pin her mother down like an animal. Her mother was too weak and bruised to resist him. Her dress torn, her spirit hunted down, she lay limp and still under him. Nancy and Bobby had been hiding in the dark corners of the house, but the drunken yells and the splintering crashes got worse.

Then the silence, most terrifying. She needed to see what that silence was. She crept out with Bobby close behind her. She saw.

Him pulling out his dink like he was going piss on her mom. Red fury whipped around her; she shrieked at him. Pounced on him with all her being. He toppled easily. Bobby pulling at his mother to get away. Her mother came back to life, pulling at Nancy to get away. But Nancy stood entranced at the door and watched her father shit-faced, struggling to his knees, his thing hanging out of his pants. He bent forward and started to pee. Nancy tried to let go, but no matter how hard she tried, she couldn't be pulled away from the filth of him flooding her senses.

THE PORNOGRAPHIC VS. THE EROTIC

Nancy learned to get along really well on the outside. She learned how to ask for things. And where to get them. She learned to pick and choose from among the giveaways. Which ones had strings attached, which ones didn't. All these things, she learned early. Because the ghosts of women taught her well. Protect your body. Protect your sex. Protect your heart.

Gregg liked, wanted, required her to keep fresh-cut flowers all over his california stucco split level on a hillside. It had a million dollar view of the city, sprawled out, spilled out, spread-eagled under its own toxic cloud. Sunlight swarmed through the patio glass; the huge bouquets in their thin elegant vases exploded in fits of passion, raining pastel shimmer off the cathedral-like ceiling; the air was intense and fragrant; Nancy wore sunglasses to read.

Gregg asked her if she wanted a flower garden to cultivate. He told her to hire a landscaper, to put in whatever she wanted. But she wanted only cut flowers to primp and to play with. She found out about the early-morning markets for the chinese greengrocers and went before dawn to choose buckets of the freshest blooms. Like them, she bought a Styrofoam cup of steaming coffee for a quarter and haggled over price. "Where yo' store, ledy?" they asked her. For a few moments, she thought she really was what she pretended to be. Somebody who belonged to somewhere. With meaning now. A somebody with a somewhere to go.

The memory of the feel of a woman's belly carried Nancy a long way, transformed itself over many seasons in her mind. Wet or dry, soggy or parched, very hot or too hot. Fortunately, in Gregg's house, there was air conditioning. Three years she stayed with Gregg, because she didn't want to be like that. Who wants to be like that? Three years she read recipes and floated around in his pool; she drove to art classes in any one of his cars. She hardly moved, hardly breathed, as if she were in a bubble that wasn't real, wasn't going to last.

Her brother Bobby would phone up every now and again.

"Bobby!" she'd yell into the phone. "Bobby, where the hell are you? Whatcha doin' there? How much? How the hell am I going to get that much?"

Gregg was too busy being the hotshot white boy to understand. He had much too much of everything. Being unethical, he wanted more. Maybe she played the part of his slit-slut too well, purring on cue, as he nuzzled her constantly, his hands hard on her butt, suggestively brushing her nipples as he talked business buddies. Him plenty big man, plenty big heart, plenty big smarts. He secure in his cliques; she stripped bare and flayed opened by their women.

THE EROTIC VS. THE PORNOGRAPHIC

Nancy used to stare down their hatred like a rock-face about to landslide, but it didn't make for nice, candlelit chitchat at the dinner table. So, in order to please their men, the women learned to ignore each other, sneering behind the phony smiles.

Nancy wondered why she was so alien to these women. Then she found out. Where she was playing for fun, they were playing for keeps. Aah, well, then, where she could see the game through to the end, they would impale themselves on the revolving spokes. She would stay in the hole of whore. Let them go for the role of wife. They tried to disguise their motives by dressing in wishy-washy colours, in confusing tiers of ruffles and flimsy lace. In their souls they were already wrung out, prepared for mediocrity. Brazenly sexual, Nancy dressed for shock and drama. She tossed her head and aimed for pure lawlessness.

Nancy heard about one couple heading home in their car, the woman's venom unleashed.

"Bitch! What is there to say to a slant-eyed whore like that? Makes me want to puke. It's degrading enough that you make me sit at the same table as her," she said, trying to make her man sheepishly conform, if only for the moment. In fact, the guy, with his hands crawling up Nancy's arm, envied Gregg's gall. He knew well enough that Greggoboy could be kicked in the head only when he was down. While he was still on top of their cutthroat heap, it was the better part of valour to find someone else to boot. That woman was dispensable at best, particularly if she couldn't find a way to pay obeisance to the not-so-complicated order of the good ol' boys.

Gregg never knew about Nancy's little brother's death. He never wanted to know about her family, and she never offered. Bobby was the only one anyway, and Bobby couldn't keep up with her. For the life of him, he just couldn't do it.

THE REFRAIN

"Run, Bobby, run!"
   "I can't."
   "Hurry! Come on!"
   "I can't."

So he had to go and get himself killed. Maybe he killed himself. Fuck you, Bobby. Fuck you all to hell. Can she imagine? He, the timid voice that reminded her once in a while that she must have been real before, burned to a bacon crisp on some fleabitten mattress up north somewhere.

Nineteen – two years younger than she. Bobby, call me! But she hadn't heard from him in a couple of months, and that worried her because no matter how bad, how poor, how sad, they usually kept in touch every week, every two weeks, a month at most. She used to think that he was a pain in the neck, always in trouble, always broke. He never listened to her.

"Got a twenty you can lend me, Nance?"

She finally phoned the RCMP. They asked her about his teeth. Were they all rotten? Can she imagine charred remains with rotted teeth hanging in there? She remembered how he used to wake her up in the middle of the night, desperate for help. His teeth rotted out even before they grew in. She fed him adult-strength aspirins, crushed them up and stuffed them into his gaping cavities.

Her reply. Her voice clinked like ice. Like broads whose brothers barbecue themselves up are a coldhearted, mysterious lot. They have to be in order to go on in their dreamlike folds of unreality.

And then she had to go and get pregnant. Is that real? She could have had an abortion; if he knew, Gregg would have made sure she was vacuumed out. See, honey, here today, gone to Maui!

THE REFRAIN

A feverish wanting to scream deep in her throat woke her up. Nancy retched into consciousness. She had fallen asleep? She must have. She had a dream, the sensation of it horrible. She dreamed that her saliva had an infestation of fleas. Every time she opened her mouth and gave them oxygen, they came to life and sprang out of her mouth by the hundreds, wet and squirmy, onto her quilt.

She felt like vomiting, and the tension around her head made her panic. "You're safe. You're safe," she panted, wet with perspiration. Still, waves of shame washed over her. Still, she couldn't cry yet.

She felt another spasm. She looked at the clock. Two-thirty-eight. Scary. She knew she would have to go to the hospital this time for sure. Suddenly she thought of a way that Gregg would be able to find her. The hospital. Oh, so very obvious too. Any hired thug with a phone. Patient information. Ward Two south, sir. You're very welcome, sir.

She's going to be in a shadowy hospital room, see, with operating lights glaring down on her throbbing pain. All around the room, there will be wrapped bodies, masked faces, gloved hands, eyes of newt. Then she'll smell him, his cologne, his Gitanes, his newly starched clothes. He will suddenly be there in the room with her, stomping on her attempts at rebirth. He will remind her that she still has her death in front of her. She will read his terrible thoughts.

THE REFRAIN

I'm going to get you, Nancy, I'm going to fix it so you never get away from me again. How much didya embezzle off me, Nancy?

But you gave me that money. I didn't steal it.

I bought you clothes, jewellery, pleasure, toys, trinkets, knickknacks. What, am I stupid enough to pay you to dump me?

No, Gregg, bad for the ego!

Fucking rights, honey! No freedom for you, never freedom, Nancy. Go straight to jail!

Nancy lay listening. She tensed because when she heard it, she recognized it right away. Outside, below her window, along the sidewalk, the sound of a woman's high-heeled shoe scraping the pavement. Slow, the drunken, drugged, staggering beneath the anger; the footsteps of hopelessness. In fuck-me shoes. Aimless, endless, stumbling. Two-forty a.m. A hacking cough. The air cold and wet. Tonight, the night restless.

DYKE DOLLARS

SHE COULDN'T BELIEVE that her mother would fall for that pig. He lied through his teeth, and he was backlogged with shit right up to his eyeballs, but of course his perennial excuse was that he didn't realize – he belonged to the sort who generally never need to know. Too busy covering his ass to actually see where the hell he was going. But that won't last past the honeymoon. How could her mom not see, for god's sake?

"Mom, you're like totally losing it," she said the other day. "Don't you remember there was once a time when you wanted to feel totally wonderful, not just be told that you look wonderful. Mom, get a grip. I mean, would anyone at all believe that he actually pays good money for black patent shoes? To wear?"

But she ended up sounding spoiled and bratty. And her stupid mother married him anyway. She did. Just like that. Well, Monica told her in no uncertain terms that she could not, absolutely would not, live with him.

"I'd just as soon hitch a ride back to Portland and fight with Daddy's newest wife day and night." She sniffed. "At least that way I'd have a chance of keeping my food down."

In retaliation, her mother oh-so-prettily reminded her that if she wasn't a college dropout to begin with, she wouldn't have to worry about living with any of them for the rest of her life.

"Ooh, I'm scared." Her only recourse being smartass.

"Besides, I'm not asking you to live with us," said her mother. Then she packed her bags and took off to Ottawa with her Herbie. Her very own mother. Left her a pink perfumed note pinned to her pillow that said,

Dear Monica:

My darling, you are twenty years old, a young woman now, not a girl any more. It's time you learned to do for yourself. And I'm not just your mother, you know. I am a young woman myself, and I have romantic needs that cry out to be met. Herbie is a good man, and I feel he's been very patient with you. Now, you're welcome to stay in the apartment as long as you want, but I'm afraid that I had to let Mrs. Spados go. However, if you decide to go back to Portland, let me or Daddy know, and one or the other of us will wire you the airfare. But you know the situation there as well. Do think about university next term, darling.
Your loving Mom.

Monica didn't believe her. She thought for sure that her mother would turn around and be back home within two weeks. And Herbie was not a good man. He was a suck. And she hated him, and all salesmen like him. Ooh, she held out for pride as long as she could, but then came the day she ran out of cashew butter, she like totally ran out of everything. She couldn't believe that her very own mother would abandon her for yet another penis head.

Finally she got on the phone to Mrs. Spados, sputtering and blubbering about how the bathroom sink got plugged and the hall carpet got sopping wet. How she couldn't get hold of her horrible mother who had gone nuts. And how she was going to do herself in with gas because nobody in this sick world loved her.

Now Mrs. Spados knew that there was no gas in the apartment, and that she wasn't going to get paid, but she came to the rescue with two bags of groceries. These she had gotten by taking two buses across town to the one and only health-food store that Monica and her mother seemed to approve of. There wasn't money in the cookie jar to pay her back because Monica had used it all up – a haircut and eating out at vegetarian restaurants – but Mrs. Spados patiently listened to Monica sob out her reproaches against this offence and that disappointment. And when it came time to go, she took the younger woman on another city bus to the only safe place she knew, the Philippines Domestic Workers Centre.

There, the women discussed Monica's situation among themselves. There were a few poker-faced comments about not understanding what exactly was her problem, but they had all been domestics long enough to know not to so much as smile, never mind grimace, in front of white employers. They made Monica feel welcome and gave her Lily's baby to play with. Thank goodness, this seemed to entertain Monica for quite some time. And the baby seemed to like her too, so they all went back to their volunteer work of trying to scare up the pittance needed to keep their tiny centre open and humming.

While she waited for Lily to return from her errands, Mrs. Spados, who was called Sunny by her *compatriotas,* used the office telephone to ask abut two jobs advertised in the newspaper even though they didn't look promising, and she felt the usual abruption at the sound of her accent – she was lucky, she thought to herself, she was landed. Only where?

Sunny found herself loafing about in self-doubt too much these days. She never used to do this back home, but now she felt neither here nor there. Not one of them, yet not one of us any more either. She looked around and saw familiar, cheap pink plastic woven ornaments everywhere. She grew listless thinking about the dangling piecemeal lives of brown women. Not exactly welfare – more like stultifying fare. Ten years of chasing down bureaucratic decoys in this country had staled her and, worse, separated her from the newly risen golden faces who came freshly baked every day to their beloved women's centre.

Lily swooped in, briefcase in hand, and scooped up her baby, who immediately stepped up the fussing at the sight of her doting mother. Lily grinned at Monica, who blinked back as though momentarily blinded by a bright light. Then Lily wondered who was this young white woman playing with her baby? She and Sunny had a meeting planned, during which they were going to draft another proposal for funding to yet another bureaucrat. Sunny had agreed to speak about her group's needs, and Lily had volunteered to write it up in proper good jargon on her laptop.

"So who's the white kid?" Lily asked the back of Sunny's head, point-blank, making her lurch back in her chair as Lily snickered. She was a lawyer, looked chinese but acted brash.

Sunny explained who Monica was, and Lily immediately seemed to lose interest, gazing into the drunken face of her infant at her breast.

The afternoon wore on. Their letter was finally finished, except Lily decided to use the big computer at the *Her Rising* office a few blocks up the Drive. She asked Monica if she felt like taking a stroll with her. Monica did not hesitate at all. Sunny looked relieved. And Lily felt very pleased with herself for again doing the right thing.

On their way Monica admired her own reflection in every storefront. She looked like a gangly little girl with impossibly narrow hips in jeans with a three-digit price tag, who just happened to stand a head taller than Lily, who is of no mean height herself. With Monica sporting a toy stroller with a real-live china doll in it, Lily managed to extrapolate all kinds of

information from an amazing number of dispassionate un-
knowns in Monica's past.

To Lily's many inquiries, Monica replied, "I dunno." Except
when Lily asked what she would wear if she were a murderer,
wanting to pull the wool over the judge's eyes.

"Oh, that's easy," she answered with a surprisingly well-
thought-out answer: "I'd wear my mom's white linen blouse
that she got from Japan. It's got the sweetest, sexiest scoop neck
and ruffles along . . . "

Lily's professional assessment was fast and dirty – too young,
a bit numb-stunned, vain and silly, your honour, but basically a
nice and a bit smarter than usual white kid.

As they passed the bookstore, Lily wanted to see if anyone
she knew was about, so she ducked in to buy a copy of the *New
Internationalist*. Inside there was a crowd, and the baby woke
up and looked entirely undecided about the deluge of strangers
around her. However, Monica picked her up and showed her
an array of brightly coloured slogan buttons on the wall. Lily,
waiting in line, admired the two of them together, and tried to
fix for all time the image of her baby wrapped in Monica's
freckled toothpick arms, just barely consoled to within an inch
of her very short and yet absolutely meaningful life.

"Lily, I haven't seen you at our place in ages," said a propul-
sive voice behind her. She turned around and there was Barb,
the managing editor of *Her Rising* staring straight at her, cracking a whiplike smile, and continuing to plough right along.

"We've been so busy and really short on help. I mean, where
is everyone? What's the new wave now? It sure as hell ain't the
collective spirit any more. Everywhere the walking wounded –
this one's bummed out, that one's freaked out. But where does
that leave the magazine?"

At first Lily felt like telling her to back out of her face. But
then, for no good reason other than Barb's chronic complain-

ing, Lily began to see humour in her situation. She felt a wave of affection towards Barb, and imagined that if she had a canada-goose feather in her hand, she would have tickled Barb's fleshy pink ear to death.

"Quite honestly, Barb," Lily said, "dinosaur to dinosaur – and you may well remember we have had this little discourse before – don't you think that there is perhaps more relevance in asking not what women can do for the published word, but rather what exactly does the process of publishing jargon do for women? Or is that sedition in these harsh and unfunded times?"

"Oh, Lily, fuck off," replied Barb as if she had just remembered. Barb's attention slid over to Monica, which gave Lily an idea.

"Your nanny?" Barb inquired in a cutting tone.

"Monica, Barbara. Barbara, Monica. And no to your obnoxious question," Lily answered crisply. "As a matter of fact, we were actually on our way to the office to see you, Barb. I just dropped in here to buy a rag or two. Do you want to walk back to *Her Rising* with us?"

"No," replied Barb with a deliberate, accusatory pause, "I have a million and one things to do. The deadline for the new issue was last Friday, but Kathy the typesetter has just disappeared. And you remember Elizabeth, at the printing press, don't you?"

"Your friend Elizabeth? Yeah, how is she?" Lily felt afraid to ask.

"The pits. Her postpartum depression hasn't let up. I think it's gotten worse. She's suicidal, you know. She can't be left alone, her mood swings are so bad. And her partner is absolutely useless. Moss told me she wanted out. I yelled at her. I really did. I said to her, 'Can't you hold off on your own effing needs until we get her through this one?' And do you know what she said? She said that it wasn't her fault, that she didn't ask Elizabeth to get knocked up again."

"Where are her kids? Three now, right?"

"They're with Wendy and what's-her-name. The baby, too, sometimes."

Barb did look tired. Lily thought she looked both over-inflated and oh so collapsible. Barb took a deep breath, realized that she was being examined and narrowed her expression to a basic snarl. "Now, what did you want of me?"

"Now, now, tsk, tsk, Barbara, I know you are majorly stressed, but what an attitude, eh?" Lily glanced coyly at the white woman and saw red. "Well, I wanted to give you something that might help you out. That's all. You wannit? Or not?"

So when it came time for Elizabeth to answer the knock at the door of her basement suite, her good friend Barb managed a comforting smile at her and a grateful one back at Monica, who smiled blandly at Elizabeth, who did not smile back at all. Soon after that, Barb left Monica with Elizabeth, with the cryptic explanation that Elizabeth needed someone to help her keep it together, for a while. And here is a list of phone numbers just in case.

"Is she going to do something . . . like, aah . . . ugly?" quizzed Monica in all innocence.

"No, no, of course not. No," answered Barb emphatically. "But, there are tons of people on that list I gave you. Listen, kiddo, I swear I won't be long."

"I really love your place. It's so cosy," Monica effusively offered up to Elizabeth, who lived in a hole and at the end of her fuse. She was again in mourning, in fear, in hell. She hated these depressive episodes. Her hormones let her down. No, her life let her down. No, she hated her mother, and now her sleazebag of a girlfriend had shafted her too.

"Heeeyy, I really hate mine too," contributed Monica with youthful zeal.

Elizabeth, or Bitsy to her friends, looked at Monica and knew right away that it wasn't the same kind of exhaustive hate at all. Not that Bitsy was up to discussing it with her. At first, the older woman thought, Who is this twit that Barb brought, but right away the twit asked if she could do the dishes or something to help out. Yeah, thought Bitsy, it's real good she knows how to keep herself entertained. Because Bitsy needed time to herself. Lots of it. To think. To nervously flick ashes from her cigarette into her ashtray. And to stare morosely at nothing in front of her.

Once upon a time, and Bitsy did mean once, her mother put a pink ribbon on her fine baby curls, called her Bitsy Witsy, took a photo and then ditched her like nothing at all. It was a name she has never been able to live down, perhaps because she has made the same dumb mistake of fondly divulging it to her lovers in the heat of each of her flaming love affairs. But with each awful, nasty breakup, Bitsy got a little more tight-lipped about who she is.

Thank goddess for friends like Barbara. And it's like comic relief not to have to get involved with her as a lover as well. Love is screwed, thought Bitsy, which not very surprisingly led her to her next idle thought, which was: Well, then, love is also screwing people, and screwing around, and ultimately getting screwed – and Bitsy was sick to death of the screwups – so screw everyone!

Deep down Bitsy purled around and around her aching self-pity, but on the surface she took comfort in dealing and reading her own tarot cards out loud to Monica, who got all excited about the creative possibilities of this new game.

There was a knock at the door. Bitsy jerked up as if she had been expecting someone. But it was just her pal Wendy, with her three kids. As soon as they arrived, the two girls, Madeleine, aged three, and Josephine, aged five, began to make strange, huddling and clutching their mother while staring intently at Monica. The newborn smelled mother's milk and wailed for it.

The little kitchen with its corroded faucets and brown patches of ancient linoleum under bare light bulbs became a cosy and reassuring home front as each woman set about her own unspoken task, without imperatives, without hesitation. Life was always transforming itself. But of course they were blissfully unaware of this, busily cooking frozen peas and Kraft macaroni dinners, nursing the baby and laundering diapers.

Monica found a rice bowl to mold the waxy neon orange mixture into one perfectly smooth round mound per big dinner plate. Then she surrounded each mound with a sea of boiled green peas. She told the little girls that the macaroni was a princess's island and, after sprinkling chives on top, named those the princess's forest.

"And the peas are brave soldiers in boats guarding the princess's moat. But you have to be so, so, and I do mean so very careful not to spill any of the peas because that would mean a dead soldier, and the princess desperately needs all her soldiers to protect her against the evils of this world," Monica decreed.

Little Josephine was enthralled; her eyes popped out while she sucked in gobs of air through her puckered mouth.

"But, but" – she got so charged up that she couldn't get her words out without shrieking – "but if we eat them, then they'll die too." Her tender little lips started to quiver. Her whole demeanour gushed into earth-shattering tears.

Monica sat Josephine on a chair, and with a gentle hand, she stroked at the small girl's shoulders as if maybe she could brush off such heavy burdens. Madeleine stood mute, sucking fiercely on her thumb. Monica pulled her up onto her lap, taking care not to hold her down. Madeleine's small body stiffened, but she stayed.

"Well, maybe something else happens, Josephine," Monica suggested.

"What?" cried Josephine, whose tears dried up like a summer shower.

"Well, say, like, if you eat the princess's island, then the princess grows inside you, right? And then you gotta eat the oldiers. You know why? So that they can protect you and the princess too, OK? This is like totally awesome, serious business."

Thereafter, Monica showed them how to chase the soldiers around the moat with their omnipotent teaspoons. Without spilling, of course. And the little girls screeched with joy.

And though the grown-up girls were just as hungry for a good fairy tale, they were a bit harder to seduce. Bitsy and Wendy slouched in their kitchen chairs and listened to Monica with guarded interest. It was Wendy who not only broke the spell of the story but almost froze the peas again. And with her impenetrable makeup, black-and-blue rasta hair and full punk-mom regalia, she looked committed to her cause.

"We don't do 'princess' stories because they glorify the rich and privileged at the expense of the poor and oppressed. And they're sexist as hell as well, so we try to discourage those kinds of values in children, no matter how prevalent it is out there," Wendy stated as plain as day, with that repudiating face she uses to put newcomers in their place.

The self-satisfied smile on Monica's face slid right off. The enormity of her blunder made her cheeks sizzle. There had been only one other time when she had almost died of embarrassment, when she came to the spirited defence of an east indian girl on her volleyball team. Well, imagine her confusion when this same girl told her to mind her own bloody business. Come to think of it, that incident wasn't even a year ago. She doesn't know why she's always blowing it these days. She used to be so sweet and drippy perfect.

"Well, I was just trying to use 'princess' as a symbol for a very special and dear little girl, something that a five-year-old might understand and identify with," Monica tried to defend herself as she would have in English 101.

Bitsy saw America's little sweetheart, Monica, step into it. Lucky for her, Bitsy kind of liked her and would go a bit easier on her. However, Wendy, as bitchy tough mean as she acted, is Bitsy's pal, and that means they stick together – come hell or high water, as comrades in arms who hoard and share the same tattered notions of sanity and security. Her lover beats on her. She beats up another. These saddened mudpies they build and sling about in tempestuous fits. Then the crawling on all fours, to rub tear-streaked noses in the sticky mess that they have made. Yes, it's a rough world out there, and Bitsy is familiar with how promiscuous those rituals of self-preservation can be.

Bitsy looked down at her sleeping baby's face with her delicate drool of pearly breast milk in the soft rosy nook of her kisser. She marvelled at how something as helpless and plucked as a newborn can ever be expected to survive in these battle zones of life.

"Monica, you're pretty good with kids. Maybe you can just say 'special and dear little girl,'" she suggested with a sigh. "Maybe we don't need a symbol here at all," Bitsy appealed to Monica's compassionate and creative nature.

"Sure, OK." Monica readily agreed because it sounded like something new and possibly even innovative. Besides, it was no big deal for her.

However, the closing of this deal exhausted Bitsy right down to her bones. Again, the dead heap of her grief slid back into place. She took pills and the baby into the bedroom, and fell like a rock into an empty bed of her own making.

And with the skirmishes over, the winner and loser clearly in their place of order, Wendy and Monica of course became good friends. They sat down to their meal of "very special and dear little girl's" island and soldier peas as well. Everyone enjoyed the din that came with rolling the peas back and forth and all around the island. A lot of the soldiers got slopped right off. Little Madeleine wept for dear life because she had poured more peas over the edge of her imaginary world than she had realized. Wendy picked up individual green peas with her heavily ringed, chained and varnished red fingertips, as if to let them agonize slowly over their fates. Some of these she provocatively stuck into her macaroni-and-Agent Orange sphere, along with a story.

"On my plate, this is the great female egg, and all these are frantic little sperm guys trying to get at the egg," she said, shaking her plate so that the peas all went crazy, popping and bopping off the veritable edge, "to make a baby." She stared with deadly precision at Monica, who blushed, deeply embarrassed, to the roots of her new shave.

Josephine howled with delight at this version, and enthusiastically did as she was shown. Many more peas died in the intensity of the moment.

By the time Bitsy's lover, Moss, waltzed in unexpectedly with the heels of her cowboy boots clicking like cockroaches on the linoleum floor, the smaller girls had fallen asleep in front of the television, Barb had called an hour ago and apologized for not being able to get away, and Wendy and Monica were giggling foolishly over the videocassette sex scenes in *Henry and June*. They were getting into expanding their inventory of f-words. Wendy was friendlying up to Monica, who was very much into the flirting and frolicking.

"Feverish!" hissed Wendy, keeping her voice down, more for effect than in consideration of the sleepers.

"Frantic, frenzied, flailing," Monica bebopped right along.

"Ooh, she's a fleshy, floozy, flirt..." Wendy kept up her lead.

"But he's a fake, a fishy phallacy, a fickle fake." Monica got her own back.

"Uh-oh, meltdown fusion," sneered Wendy, who had seen the movie before.

"Delirium," murmured Monica, who had not. And this, for no reason at all, sent them rolling in hysterics around the carpet until the sighting of Moss, standing there with an odd, crooked grin on her anglo face, interrupted their mirth.

Wendy grew wary, since she knew she was supposed to snub Moss right away, but Monica, the perpetual baby-sitter, perked up, gave her a big ol' grin and said, "Hi, there."

And like a remote-control TV, Moss turned on the southern charm. She played her best supportive role by tiptoeing over to the children and tucking in the comforter, her long hands lingering on a chubby cheek or two.

She needed some time alone with Bitsy so she could explain her side of the story. But Bitsy got so hysterical and self-destructive at the sight of Moss that it took days and many more pills to calm her down, so Bitsy's friends had all agreed that Moss should not be allowed anywhere near Bitsy.

"Gee, I really love your slick cowboy boots," burbled Monica, who did not have the experience to pick up on what was really slick and what was not. Moss turned and popped a perfect saccharine smile at her.

"Why, thank you. I really fell in love with them too. I knew when I first saw them that they would either break my heart or my wallet. Do you think I made the right choice?"

Monica was charmed, but Wendy's attentions had already

strayed back to the more reliable television in the room. Before long, Moss had squeezed her way into Bitsy's bedroom. As soon as she closed the door, Wendy got up and phoned Barb, who was at the back door within a breathtaking five minutes. Instead of coming in, she signalled Wendy to come out.

Monica was beginning to get a whiff of a plot in the air, but she couldn't imagine what the fuss was about. She did some waving and tiptoeing just for a chance to ask Barb, "Do you think I should stay?"

"Yes, yes, please stay," Barb hissed at her, with a finger pressed tightly against her lips. "Monica, you've been a great help, and it's really important that you stay, OK?"

"Sure, OK," replied Monica, who was good-naturedly curious, so she went back into the thick of things and curled up in an armpitchair, with a dirty magazine called _Swish_ that she had dug up in the piles of newspapers. Peeking out the kitchen window, she could see Wendy and Barb conferring by the garage, smoking cigs.

Some time passed through this uneasy standoff, until a terrible shriek tore into the late-afternoon lull. Monica jumped to her feet, and her arms reflexively jerked up. The dirty magazine went flying, slapped the low ceiling and landed behind the girls' chesterfield. They squirmed uneasily, frowning as if concentrating on the continuation of their rightful repose. Monica hopped up and down as her heart pounded. She had never been in a situation like this. Suppose someone was being murdered. She listened to more grunts and growls, the sound of scuffling and heavy furniture being bumped and a baby's startled wail.

Moss got ejected from Bitsy's bedroom with surprising force. She did not tarry on her way out. She skidded around the corner and bumped into Barb, whose face was red. She looked puffed up, ready to stomp on the most disgusting, slimiest snake she had ever met in her entire career.

Oh, but my goodness, how time flies around here, thought Monica, who finally looked at the clock when she realized she was hungry. It was late. Bitsy was blotto on the couch, and everyone else had finally gone, though each of their emotionally charged departures still lingered in the air. Monica sat in wonderment in the kitchen, with magazines and tarot cards in front of her, laundry hanging over her head, sipping on Bitsy's wine, puffing on Wendy's rollies and getting exposed to all sorts of new ideas.

Whenever Monica got hungry, she remembered Mrs. Spados, who always seemed glad to get a call from her. Mrs. Spados asked Monica if she had just gotten home.

"No, I'm still helping Bits . . . Elizabeth out. She's a friend of Barb's" was Monica's ready reply. "I think I'm going to stay here overnight."

"What's Elizabeth's last name? What's her phone number?" Mrs. Spados wrote these down dutifully and passed along a message: "Your mother phoned me. You're supposed to call her collect. She's been wondering about you. You sure you're OK?"

"I think I'm going to be just fine, Mrs. Spados," answered Monica, who felt touched. "Don't worry about me. I'm a big girl now."

"Well, Monica, I'm happy that you remembered to phone me. I was . . . I felt kind of responsible for you, you know." Sunny's tone of voice was reassuring, but she was already flipping through her phone book, looking for Lily's number.

BLOODED IN BRAZIL

THE WITNESS

HE ALMOST GAVE UP his luxury condo with its pure-white walls and serene ocean view. He briefly entertained the notion of going all the way and never coming back, but of course he stopped himself. Instead, he made a mental note to watch himself.

He kept the place because he did his best thinking there sitting on a heavy wing chair in the centre of the empty room with his feet in the cheap socks of his other life tossed up on its matching brocade footstool. Beside him there was a beautifully preserved, carefully chosen cedar bentbox, only slightly smaller than an end table, on which he placed his cigarettes, ashtray, his glass of wine and his cellular telephone.

So he came but he didn't stay. The room looked vague and felt detached, crisscrossed by shadows, cut up into gauzy swatches of fine, shimmering pinstripes by the tall vertical blinds closed against the glare and heat of daylight. The summer sun was setting, making the darkened insides glisten. Eerie, the limbo, the latent light permeating every muted molecule of stillness within. And so he sat in this pulsating glow. Living art, he thought smugly.

THE PERPETRATOR

He thought he should have had someone in to decorate and furnish the rooms. Usually he did, even though he had never stayed in any of his places for long. He had noticed that a proper home was always more enticing than a vacant one. And he was careful to do things just right, but this time he seemed to have lost . . . a certain consistency.

All he owned was in cold storage; his car was also hidden away, parked underground. He knew that for sure. There was no need to go and see for himself. It was tightly locked and impenetrable. The security people here were very cocksure, even fastidious about property. Their material sensibilities were admirably intact, indeed unquestionably sacred.

For instance, they had been alerted to his arrival in a taxi. On their grainy video screens, they watched him walk up to his door and push the right code to get in. Then they wrote him up on their computers and cross-referenced him because he didn't look like the type that can live here. They had maybe four sightings of the "ghost tenant" in number 2224. He was a keeper, not an owner, as in happy homeowner. They wondered briefly what his line might be, but the old biddy in 1808 already wanted her doggy toileted again.

If there was ever a need, he could say, as he had done to the beautiful husband-and-wife realtor team, that he was between jobs, but then he would also add that he was not really looking either, since in his line of business, people somehow managed to find him.

"And what line of business is that, may I ask?" she had asked in her winning way.

"Recycling," he replied, cocking his head in the same funny way she did. Only she didn't laugh.

Pius – his partner in crime – someone who always manages

to find him, would remark that this kind of cockiness only arouses suspicion. However, he would argue that he had more often than not found nice people to be suspicious anyway. And this strangeness actually distracted them. The wife whispered to the husband, "God, is he ever creepy!" And sold him the place as he knew they would – a place to come to, not a place to live in.

THE PERPETUATOR TO THE WITNESS

That morning, Pius himself had come downtown to summon him. A turning bus honked impatiently at Pius, who was standing too close to the curb. Pius had his folded newspaper in hand and started whapping at the menacing bearlike bus whose tires squealed to a jerking stop. Nonplussed, Pius kept his eyes on him until he looked up to see the cause of this commotion. Their eyes met for an instant, then Pius stepped scornfully in front of the cumbrous bus, which was forced to wait, and disappeared.

Noise and ataxia of heavy metal traffic pumping past, but Pius's theatrical note was loud and clear. Rexx, what the fuck are you doing?

Well, specifically, at that particular moment, he was helping a tattered old bag lady across the one-way street of life, stopping four lanes of hostile drivers in powerful cars, who didn't feel they should have to wait for their special destinies and who probably thought nothing of running over the dirt and scum that got in their way. She was oblivious to all high-and-mighty causes, muttering doggedly to herself and waddling along, and he was behind her, attentive to and curious about all the forms of death and dying that he saw around. Her decaying pig face, her warmed-over smells of urine and her clotted wattles of filth; she was very looney, and he wanted to find out if she was as free of death as her appearance portrayed. He figured that if he poked her with a sharp stick and she shrivelled or howled, then her death was still in front of her. However, if there really was no response, then her death was behind her. And she was definitely free. And that's the best kind of helping he could think of, wasn't it?

And generally these days he's been busy making himself the most available volunteer suck this seedy, needy, downtown neighbourhood has ever had – his hair in a squirt of a ponytail, wearing a pair of baggy green work pants and a red down vest over a wrung-out turquoise T-shirt, and calling himself Tony. He fit right in. Tony here. Tony there. Tony everywhere. He liked being Tony. Tony having coffee, smoking cigarettes at Betty's restaurant with some of the guys from VETO, Vancouver Eastside Tenants Organization. They were great big grunting patriarchal commie lugs who talked AA incessantly and patrolled their streets aggressively. At night, with their beach-ball bellies, they delighted in bouncing hookers, their johns and their pimps and their druggies "the hell out of our neck of the woods."

Of course, he couldn't really feel it, but it was apparently a good thing to be a contributing member of the community. They liked him, towered above him, assumed that he stayed in one of the flophouses nearby.

"No problem, Tony." They had decided that he could move into any one of the subsidized housing "coops" they had around here. No questions asked. No past. Tony liked that. No future. He liked that too.

"You look like our kind of rooster," they crowed and crowed.

Beside him, the cellular phone rang.

"You look like a fuggin' diesel dyke," Pius warned soon as he called. "You've gone soft. You haven't done one in a long time, and you've gone soft." Then he heaved a sigh.

Rexx grinned stupidly at the phone.

Onceuponatime he told Pius that he was retiring, but of course Pius could not believe him. In their game nobody retires his self.

"Listen, Rexx," Pius said at the time (that brutal mafioso act Pius puts on just about kills Rexx every time), "the business we do ain't very pretty. I nose ya need ta relax a bit, you know, enjoy yaself like everybody else. Sure, sure go ahead. Take a breather, whaddya say?"

Then about a year later, Pius phoned again, and said, "Ya know, Rexxy baby, with any other guy, I'd just offer more money. But I already know it ain't money that turns you on."

Rexx laughed because he understood that there were only limited avenues of communication left open to them – to anyone for that matter – and great tracts of human being left untouched. He enjoyed Pius. As a pimp – they called them pimps too – Pius was more personable than the others who made what Rexx did even more unsavoury with their furtive, grim, hard-core faces up his ass.

They used to sicken him, approaching him with their obscene offers of money and more money. At the same time, they hated him because he had the balls and could ask for anything he wanted, and they would comply. But they never knew that it wasn't the money. It's never the money. Money was just an act, a symbol to him. They don't have a goddamn clue what actually motivated guys like him to kill for them.

Now Pius – he didn't know if Pius knew either, but he knew that Pius knew there were a lot of guys who were pretty hit and miss out there. That was why he called every once in a while to ask, "Well, Rexxy, you still just about the cleanest guy I know, and who knows, you may be up for another one?"

"No," he would say.

"You're kidding." Pius would be more than disappointed. There would be a loaded pause on the phone pointed at his head, and Pius would very carefully say, "Then you don't even want to hear about it?"

Rexx might deign to say "Sure, I'll listen."

He never knew. It could have been something that surprised him for a change, but it wasn't. Another foreign or domestic nobleman wanted to knock off his pregnant wife. And it was essential that the catholic church didn't know, har-dee-har-har. To him now Brazil seems not so much harder to get back to, but hardly worth his time any more.

But today, suddenly, there it was – a couple of seconds' too long a pause, then came the vicious snarl that he had been instinctively expecting from Pius for a long time: "You'd think that you would have had your fun with your little monkey cunt by now."

"You'd think," his sprung reply, as his spine tightened and arched; his lips pulled back in a leer. So Pius found out. Pius done went out and did his homework. Fucking tracked him with a vengeance. And now Pius was outraged.

"It's been three years now, Rexx. You know, a few of the guys have been asking after you. And I know that tough guys like you and me can't stand to lose our edge. So what can I tell them – that you lost your nerve?"

"Tell them to mind their own goddamn business," he growled, knowing that Pius knew better than to try to suck him into a discussion like this. But it was just protocol, after all. Someone steps outta line, he's gotta be tried and executed. It was the ritual, and he didn't expect mercies. And Pius wasn't going to give any. This was, in fact, a telephone survey, a playful foray to see if there were any telltale signs of ooze or corrosion. Pius was just doing his job. Well, then, so was he. Just doing his joust. Real fun and games can go in either direction.

"You wanna be cunt meat, Rexxy?" Pius asked, panting. "Well, I'll be glad to stick it to ya. I sure doan like to find out that you been copping out on me three years now. Makes an awful fool of me, donnit."

"Yeah, well, love wounds forever, you big prick. So come and throw me a retirement party, if you can." As he turned off the receiver and neatly smoked another one, he realized that he quite enjoyed the spiritual absoluteness of what he did.

THE WITNESS TO THE PERPETUATOR

He remembered that his mark was a skinny kid with a chalky-white face and blistering black eyes. Her head was covered, and she had a tiny, swaddled bundle in a corduroy carrier tied to her chest. Every other day she scuttled out to the Sunrise market for the day's supply of bean curd and vegetables. On frosty mornings when it was still dark and foggy, she shivered her scrawny butt off. Pitiful. He imagined he could smell the fear on her.

The mewling newborn in the synthetic fleece was what turned him off. She passed by without noticing him in the shrubs. The switchblade up his sleeve was just long enough for her. Nobody had mentioned any kid to him. He caught up to her by a concrete wall. Left rubber-gloved hand could have closed her throat, while the right played heart surgeon. A couple of flicks of the wrist. He would feel her slump, then he'd reach in for her billfold and be across the street before her head flounced off the pavement. But he hated leaving debris. And he especially hated other people's careless litter. He passed her. She gasped at how close he came. She jerked back. And he strode right by her, eyes dead set ahead – a guy in a brown bomber jacket and a blue knit skullcap, his air Nikes silent as bat wings, his work very clean. It should have been so smooth; a badly shaken vegetable peddler might have been the only witness. I don't know, officer, he not too short, not too tall.

He knew he had left her with her heart hammering in her

chest. Her woollen mitts covered her trembling mouth, which heaved out her breath and sucked in the freezing mist. He knew how exposed she felt. How reduced to absolutely nothing. The baby at her breast slumbered on. She peered down at it, then looked all around, at the chill, at the empty streets. He knew that she must have felt crazy.

That was three years ago. So now her child stared back at him with entirely different eyes. She didn't smell bad. She didn't have to eat shit. She didn't have a hungry ferocity about her mouth, not the soullessness before her teeth even grew in, none of the dreadful sores. He didn't kick ashes to bury her squalid remains in this fenced-in playground.

She piped up, in all-knowing innocence, and asked, "Did you come from far away?"

"Yes," he answered with a gentle voice, "I was blooded in Brazil." He was so close that he reached out and stroked her chubby cheek. She moved away.

"Why are you here?" Her voice tinkled like a tiny glass bell.

"Because I want to tell you not to cry."

"My mommy says it's all right to cry," she shrieked at him with delight, somersaulting her small body over the very idea.

Her mother was immediately by her side. She hated him. As softly as he tried, she had never liked him.

"What did you say to her?" she asked point-blank, offensively.

"Oh, hi there, Deedee." He smiled at her with exaggerated enthusiasm. "You know what? You're just about the most paranoid person I have ever met. How'd you ever pick up a name like Deedee anyway? I have a cousin named Deedee and she's just about the friendliest person I know."

Her eyes flashed at him, hesitant for an instant. Then she saw that he saw, and she slapped on a smile, more like a sneer to cover up.

"And I have a cousin who calls himself Tony, and he was a bona fide creep too."

"Oh, bitchy, bitchy," he returned.

"You know," she said, "I've complained to the committee about people using the day-care door as an entryway, but really nobody does it except you. In fact, I've noticed that nobody sneaks all over the complex quite like you do, Tony."

"Oh, got your eye on me, do you?" He winked, but her face was immutable stone. "Well, I've got some VETO posters that I think I am entitled to hang on the bulletin board. That is, if anybody is ever allowed in to read them. And I do fix toys for the kids around here. Some of the more well-adjusted mothers in this co-op seem to appreciate that."

She turned on her heel and signalled the end of the most heartfelt conversation he has had with this woman who cowers in fear for her life and is as phony as he is in this life. Her real name is Nancy Wong, all the more grown up, confident and enticing, but no more appreciative of the three years of living on time borrowed from him.

Her little girl dragged Nancy by the hand over to the jungle-gym set. There she crawled into a barrel and demanded that she be turned round and round, squealing with all her heart. Nancy stood by her, looked back at him, not bothering to conceal her annoyance.

She wears glasses now, so that she can be more watchful, doubling, tripling, quadrupling her valiant efforts to protect her tight-ass little enclave against a big, bad motherfuckin' world out there. The way she filled up with futile detailing a life that wasn't ever hers made him want to laugh. Not at her but at himself. For being clever. Clever enough to have vision. Vision enough to know that he is blind. And trapped by the perversity of not ever being able to live without killing.

But tonight, he will finally tell her how much he wants to

gaze upon creation, as she does. He knows that she does; he has been watching her. Tonight will be an evening no different from any of her evenings. Tai chi class within her confines, taught by Mr. Lin in the multipurpose room. Then she comes back, feeds, bathes the child and lets her noisily tottle back and forth until they both become cranky with exhaustion. Usually the child crawls onto the mother's lap, lifts a T-shirt and plants an angelic mouth on one of the tawny-tipped twin peaks she finds beneath. Then it's sweet dreams for the little one while Nancy sits down at her drawing table. Night is the time when she soars far and deep into pure space where there is no matter, her face glowing beside a cheap forty-watt desk lamp.

So tonight he will tell her that she was not easy to find in the beginning. Indeed, she had been so avid about staying alive that he had sympathized and thought she deserved the chance to play out her little drama. He thought she was brilliant, and he especially loved the very professional way she cleaned out her boyfriend and vanished without a trace.

He will explain that for him, his work demands more concentration than penetration. He doesn't know how to explain it. It isn't personal; it's as if he's a conduit for something larger than himself, something huge and obscene and terrible, with a cruel violent nature that cannot be contained or denied. And each of the deaths have felt like implosions, harder and harder. Imagine all life's chaos, he will advise her, sucked into a black hole that doesn't exist, never did and never will.

He will use light bright scarves and soft silk ties because he wants to see how they will look against her tortured skin. He will talk to her as seductively as another woman, mesmerizing her into unfurling her petals towards his radiance, his mouth gentle, tasting wherever his fingers touched lightly her curves and slopes. And the child would dream on.

THE END

So that night he bent over her and breathed in her scent. It was a hot night in the inner city when the sweat between her skimpy breasts gleamed, and the long black tendrils of wet hair stuck on her neck and shoulders. She fell asleep with her music playing, her murder mystery from the library slumped on the floor, her glass of wine empty, tipped over. Her baby has long ago learned to climb out of her own crib and into her mother's bed, curling fetal tight against her belly.

The bathroom lights were left on. Carelessly. Purposely. Splashy, exotic underwear was suspended over the bathtub, which was filled with a drenched variety of potted plants. The child's bedroom doubled as a sewing room with a real-live department-store dummy secured to the wall, half dressed and smiling and staring. Toys booby-trap the hallway.

Her diary, her photos, her drawings, her books clutter the kitchen cum living room cum office cum studio space. The kitchenware, expensive and plentiful, was tucked into every available corner and has taken over the closet as well. She has learned to preserve her own food. Specially built shelves overflowed with colourful glass jars; no labels. The oversized pressure canner had to be suspended from the ceiling on a chain with rubberized handles. The green tail of a nose-down plush animal stuck out of it.

Her whole life was holed up in this apartment cell in a subsidized housing co-op where she thought she was safe. He read in her diary:

Tuesday, July 7. The guy at Bau-Xi phoned up, and said two of my paintings good as sold. I so excited, but then I got totally depressed. Always two steps forward, twenty stumbles back.

Wednesday, July 8. It's so hot I don't feel like doing anything. Was going to go to the wading pool with Cat, but really, can't even venture out that far. Landed up sitting in Memphis's junky apartment all afternoon, smoking. Her kids climbing the walls. At least she has a breeze. Could have biked. Too dangerous for Cat without a baby-sized helmet. Can't find one in this part of town. Details, goddamn absurd details all the time. Gets to me. But Cat sure don't seem care one way or another.

Thursday, July 9. Laundry took so long, because at least half of the stupid machines on the blink. Finally got up the nerve to phone Su Fay. Of course the phone rang and rang. Why do I bother? She doesn't give a shit about me. I just need somebody's touch. I cry when I remember our time together. Did it really happen? Why do I fucking do this to myself?

That was the last entry. And he was afraid that he would find nothing to ignite him, after all. Then he turned, and he found himself staring at her photos and drawings of wildflowers, his mouth agape. Surprised then shocked. Something within him seemed to lurch out of place. Down in his gullet, he felt an old familiar putrid rawness threaten from his gut. He had to clamp down hard to keep from losing it.

On top, the first one he lit up with a blinding beam of his halogen flashlight – he thought it was splashes of vermilion blood on what must have been slit-mottled flesh. It looked so vivid. He steadied his hand and made himself look again. No, they were just flowers. Weird and twisted wildflowers with velvety calyxes, viciously red, done in shivering wet nail polish, bursting out of the deep crevice of a powdered dry, leathery canyon rock-face.

He looked again, leering at the painted picture's shamelessness. Yes, there was a lewdness in the strokes. The fascinating freshness, the corruption between the bursts of scarlet, and the dirty flesh – yes, he was not mistaken after all. It was filthy, the way she drew out of the foliage, straddling and strangling the duller plants nearby, as if devouring them. He did not need to look any more.

He stood in the dark, feeling as he had felt the very first time he was blooded. In Brazil, where they showed him how they pick off the street children for bounty, and how they leave their scrawny black bodies, but not the heads, to the wild dogs in the streets. It was an aching, engorged fascination with his own revulsion at his own life.

CROSSWALK MAN

(for Nathan)

I WANT TO TELL YOU a story about a sign of life that really happened. Indeed, it could have happened right under any of our very unhappy noses in any of our crowded and irritated cities. But it did not happen overnight; only after many years of pondering did he finally peel loose and glide gently onto the ground without cracking, or splitting or flaking. All his parts intact. I talk about the little crosswalk man with his perfectly circular head, his stick body with sturdy arms and one leg straight and the other provocatively bent.

"The ego has landed," he said to himself because he had once heard these words and admired their grandiosity. He didn't really understand their meaning. Having been secured to a light post at a busy intersection just above the heads of passersby all this time, he had overheard millions of snatches of conversation and had had to piece together much of what he knows. Well, listen at any street corner for yourself, and you will better understand!

"Karen, sweetheart, willya wake up and smell the coffee and cigarettes? She's getting far too fat. This wouldn't be happening if you stayed home and picked up a frying pan once in a blue moon."

"Mommy, Mommy, I'm bored. Can we go to McDonald's?"

"It's this way."

"I say it ain't.

"Is."

"Ain't."

"Fuck off and die, you whore."

No, it's not as if he got things nicely explained to him. Nobody ever really noticed him. Whenever they did look up, it was because they were frantically searching for street names or directions to the freeway or because they were cursing bitterly at the red light. Mothers walking their small children sometimes took notice and stopped to grin at him in delight. That was how he got his name, "the little crosswalk man." But lately there were fewer and fewer sightings of him and them. The people had mostly been scared away, and the ones who did walk along here because they had to, were too scared, tired or defeated to stop and point him out to their little ones, who would smile their beatific first understanding at him. Really, they would. They look as if they want it . . . need it so badly too.

Ah, but it was nobody's fault in particular. Everybody had gotten drowned out by the clank and roar and grind of never-ending traffic. He once told me that he felt himself to be the most useless, pedestrian, unseen sign of our times. Well, surely to dog, I could understand how that would be enough to make a sensitive little stick man shy.

Well, anyway, there he was newly rebirthed, still quivering and quaking. Right away he hid beneath a parked car, and right away it moved. Poor little guy. He didn't quite know what to do, but he felt that it wouldn't have been proper for a little crosswalk man to be seen running about on his own in broad daylight. I personally think that it would have made some people sit up and take a bit more notice, but he didn't want any trouble.

He managed to wobble his way into a very discreet and dark place under a garbage container on the sidewalk. That's where I found him. I ambled along, thought he was just another thin paint job, gave him a disinterested sniff, pissed on him and presented him with an entirely other perspective. And why not? Who am I but some dog out on the streets looking for shit to eat? As it turned out, he was open and friendly, and we were both quite the philosophical fellows.

Movement was a new experience for him, even though he has been a flawless symbol for movement for as long as he could remember. But he had done so only by staying obediently and sublimely still on his firm, reflective surface. His worldview from up there had been very different from his current situation, and I could tell he was frightened. He kept glancing, in fact, gazing longingly back at what used to be a safe place for him – and was now a flat, blank square that had lost its meaning.

"There," he said, "I had form, purpose and structure, and even superstructure."

"So why did you leave, then?" I scratched my woolly neck. Although I thought he was being a bit of a crybaby, I could also understand his point about losing one's background. That can be a very intimidating, even traumatic, experience. Why, imagine if someone came along and reversed my dog identity, then turned me into some kind of a glorified token, eh?

As I plopped myself down to doze a bit, which I do not like to do at this particular intersection with its toxic fumes and pandemonium, he divulged his story of how he came to consciousness. He used to be perfectly content with his station in life, until one day, years back, this young man happened to look up.

"Hey, man," greeted the young man when he noticed the crosswalk man, "you a good-looking dude."

The crosswalk man was surprised and glanced about. But there was nobody else around. The young man seemed very nice. He stood right underneath the crosswalk man and spoke to him as if he were a real person. He appeared to be in no particular hurry, and even paused rather than shout above the traffic noise. Back in those days, there could be as much as a ninety-three-second lull in traffic, depending on the time of night.

The crosswalk man straightened up a bit and grinned back politely. He wanted to appear friendly but wasn't ready to give up his strong, silent image.

"You know, most people would think that I have totally lost it," said the young man, "but I have just crossed over spiritually, you know, to the other side. I have tried to explain this to people, but they don't seem to get it. They get all uptight and scared, and then they do the weirdest things. I don't think they really want to know anything really important because it might bust open their heads. Or, worse still, change their minds or something subversive like that."

The crosswalk man was amazed. Not only did he understand what the young man meant, but he was also deeply moved by his words.

The young man went on, "But, man, as soon as I laid eyes on you, I knew you would understand right away. You just about the friendliest thing I've seen all day, bro. You, man, are my guiding light."

Uh-oh, I thought, but reserved comment. But of course the crosswalk man fell for it. He told me he felt a prickling and a buckling beneath his feet. And that was the first suggestion of his . . . his awareness. Merely outlined, perhaps. Maybe even a bit sketchy and superficial. Nonetheless, it was a significant genesis.

"Jeez, where am I?" the young man had asked. "I don't

usually have to go this far afield from . . . from where I usually am, I mean. But I think I've got people after me. They want to lock me up, and I don't want to go back there.

"Oh, don't get me wrong. My folks are nice enough. Really. They just ignorant and real stubborn about it. You see, to them life is a neat square box with neat square slots to it. You know, a slot for being a kid, a slot for being a father, a slot for being a wife, a slot for being rich. And anything else is a mean, ungrateful son of a bitch. And the old man would rather kill me than let me do that to my sainted mother. You know – the same old tired shit and they're never going to stop trying to kill me. Imagine if they ever did, man, they'd have to start living themselves. What a hoot! Well, gotta run. Man on the run. You like the Beatles? See ya later, man."

Oh yes, I do believe that the young man did in fact say that he would see the crosswalk man again. Just as I could see with my very own very streetwise eyes how much the poor twit had taken those words to simple heart.

"Who do you think you are?" I tried barking at him. "It's too harsh out there for types like you with nothing except a high-gloss veneer." But he didn't see himself like that at all. If he did, he probably would have crumbled long ago.

When night fell, he felt it was safe to start his quest to find this young man. At first, his steps were faltering but then he picked up speed. I followed along. Beside us, a steady stream of automobiles with hearts of steel rushed along a paved ribbon that sliced through a confusing landscape full of debris.

We saw no one until we got to the next major intersection. There, who should we meet but another well-lit little crosswalk man. This one was older, on a bright blue background. He was wearing clothes and had the cutest little fedora on his head. My crosswalk man stood in front of him and did a jaunty skip backward and forward, side to side. Bent leg. Straight leg. Bent.

Straight. He twirled around and around at top speed. Stood on his head, of course. I sensed he had a big effect on the other. Before we hit the road again, I thought I saw the tiniest bubble on his painted surface too. Right on, I thought to myself. Hang loose.

The crosswalk man got pretty good with his moves. He swooshed through the velvety-warm night air, holding on to a swing in a park, in the dark. On the next upswing, he let go and flung himself into the air. The gentle breeze carried him sailing over the roof of a low-lying building. Mind you, he had to swim a little to get beyond a tall wire fence, but when he did, he let himself swoop and land, sleek as a paper airplane, on soft, manicured lawn. That was fun, he said, and lay there for a while, one flat side looking up at the light of the moon, and the flip side burying his face in the ticklish tangle of sweet-smelling grass. He rippled with delight.

I was chuckling myself when we both heard a grunt. Or something. It wasn't a pleasant sound, whatever it was. And it had come from the direction of the playground. There was rustling in the shadows of the jungle gym. Another strangulated squawk scared the crosswalk man. He ran for tree cover and watched. Two figures in awkward positions seemed both fused to, and struggling against, each other.

"You love that, bitch?" asked one, belabouring the other.

"Ooh, fuck me to death, darling," begged the other.

No matter how flawed his original motive, I had to admire the way the little guy kept streaking effortlessly from one dimension to another. I, being a dog, did not have the same access. Or in other words, no dogs allowed. I could only wait while he jumped into a huge pool of water to marvel at its whole new iridescent way of being. He had no trouble learning to manouevre in this murky fluid realm, but suddenly a great heaving current churned him about, flipping him over and over, threatening to shatter him into small bits. That was when he came face to face with such a massive floating creature he could not even bring himself to believe in its suave black-and-white existence. It was the aquarium's killer whale, I informed him.

"And the quick-witted torpedo fish?" he asked.

"Dolphin," I replied.

Well, he was sure he had come face to face with the absolute.

And I'll bet the lively dolphin with its zip code of behaviour thought he was the best invention since herring roe too. Comparatively, he said, the whale seemed quite morose; it kept brooding and swirling its own bitter brew in its vast vat. Afterall, the potential miracle of it had been captured and installed in a display case for those blinkered humans. Imagine a gorgeous whale like that, I sighed, reduced to somebody's very odd idea of a souvenir joke.

The crosswalk man implied that he understood. But I wondered if he really did see. He was like that whale, a symbol with more potential than the real thing. Aah, he thought he was looking for a beautiful young man, but I knew he was searching for something that existed only in his imagination.

Soon after that, the crosswalk man began to care less and less about human doings seeing him. The human version of looking and seeing were two very disconnected things. For instance, he walked as cockily as he pleased past two well-heeled office girls waiting for a bus. They watched him with surprise on their faces.

One said, "I didn't see that. Did you see that?"

"No," answered the carbon copy of the other, "I didn't see that at all." They stared after him.

After a while, the first one dared to ask, "Well, how come you were able to not see what I didn't see either?"

"I dunno. But there's something fishy going on here."

"Hey, I betcha someone is having one over on us." They both peered hither and thither.

"Look for a hidden camera," suggested the more determined of the two.

Hey, let me tell you, these two were the liveliest of the bunch. By the time the bus came they had a good laugh. And I had a canine urge to yawn at my own revelation that humans are unshakable in their crude belief in their own disconnectedness. Ho hum, so what if they refuse to acknowledge the crosswalk man? That would only cause confusion and nervous breakdowns. And I could plainly see with my own doggone eyes that humans are messed up enough.

The end of the crosswalk man's quest turned out to be much more spectacular than I would have guessed. When he slithered into a 7-Eleven convenience store to browse through magazines, all seemed very ordinary. Boys of different shapes and sizes were pressed up to the video machines. A variety of mountain bikes and boy-toy cars were piled in the parking lot. People came in and out hurriedly, compulsively exchanging small bills for little boxes, even though this didn't seem to make them much happier.

Suddenly the video arcades lost all their mesmerizing high-tech attraction for the boys. In the unflinching fluorescent flood of store lights, there was absolutely no mistaking a real-live cartoon figure bent in study over a *True Love* magazine. The crosswalk man soon found himself confronted by an underaged posse of huge galoots who had plenty of smarts but absolutely no souls – of that, I, the mangy cur at the saloon doors, am sure.

And then the crosswalk man had to have his fun too. He did a fancy flip, not too high in the air, and landed lightly on his head. An audible intake of breath attended a fair amount of excitement, consternation, even panic. By now the cashiers, the new immigrant ones who never stay at this sort of exploitative job long enough to be really familiar with their environment, were alerted as well. But as usual, the grown-ups had a lot more difficulty focusing on the crosswalk man. They kept looking for a man with a gun, or at least an image problem more relevant to their own situation.

I blame myself entirely. I saw the boys power up. I saw how fantasy and reality collided in their pinball eyes, all aglow with the computerized hallucinations of an ultimate search-and-destroy mission. Each kid was a walking, twitching arsenal. I should have barked or something but I turned chicken, felt cowed as they manoeuvered themselves into strategic positions around him. With lightning speed, they were upon him with their big ugly hands. He sprang with everything he had, but one fellow got a hold, and the crosswalk man cracked under his fleshy, sweaty touch. Stunned that he had actually sustained damage, he spun and catapulted clear across the room with the help of the blasts from the air-conditioning vents.

The crosswalk man's last resort turned out to be the back of a huge, grinding Slurpee machine. But even this heavy metal monster machine did not prove sufficient protection from those swarming ten-year-olds still frenzied by their near kill. Their dank human hands kept groping towards him. He had to co-coon behind more pipes. They tried flushing him out with hockey sticks and flashlights. When some of them tried pulling the Slurpee maker from the wall, thank dog they were foiled by the store clerk, who seemed to have the upper hand.

An argument ensued – an onslaught of fast and dirty juvenile street talk against one rather awkwardly displaced adult.

"You're crazy, mister. You can't just let it fucking stay in there."

"Yeah, mister, it might be dangerous, you know? Didn't you even see it, mister?"

"I dunno. I dunno what was dat. I dunwanna no trouble. I dunwanna no stuff smashed. No trouble here."

"Mister, you've got big, big trouble. And it's right here behind this here machine. And it's against the law to let it stay there. You knowa da english, mister? Duhh, you know the law of the land? Fucking darkie."

"Hey. I dunwanna hear dat. What you wanting to buy? You kids pay your money or go out immediately, see? I dunwanna no trouble in here, or I am calling the policeman."

"OK, OK, call the cops. Go ahead. Call the cops. You said you're going to call the cops. Whatsamatta? You toad? That thing in there is a danger to society, an alien, a foreigner, so call the fucking cops."

"You call cops."

"OK, let me use your phone!"

"No way, man. You use the pay phone outside, see."

"Awww, mister? Hey, mister . . . mister? Awww, you aliens are all alike, man. Ya all stick together, doncha? I ain't buying no more drinks from that fucking machine. That's for sure. It's probably all mutagenic sludge by now."

Sick at heart, I receded into some bushes and waited until the kids went home for dinner. Finally the poor defeated bugger limped out in a traumatized daze. He told me to take him back, so I draped him over my back and carried him to his street corner. There he hung himself back up. I tried my clumsy best to make him feel better about himself. I tried to tell him that we are all misunderstood in this life. And nobody ever sticks his neck out any more. At least he tried. So what if he had a minor setback. I mean, what did he have to lose? He was all in the mind, after all. But everything I whined came out wrong. What could I tell him anyway? Not to take those brats to heart? That he had the spirit, just not enough substance?

I wagged my tail as encouragingly as I could, but I felt his loneliness with absolute clarity. We're both very tired, we told each other. I was tired of living. Maybe he was tired of not being able to die. Maybe that's the same thing. Sadly I watched him shut down, his little body suspended motionless, drenched in the misty rain. But, as I staunchly told myself, there's no room in our lives for such sentience, is there? So I doggedly moved on, because it was already getting so dark so early.

$\mathcal{W}$INTER TAN TOO

Errol Spiridigliozzi strained with all his might against the immense pressure that threatened to crush his chest against the control panel. But he could not lift a finger to save himself. The ship kept spinning out of control like a punctured balloon, speeding through time and space as if there was no matter. His face was pinned against the cold metal and rigid polymers; his mouth was forced to kiss the red blowout button, which flashed crazily back at him. The entire board wailed the ship's distress and the fact that he was living the pure chaos of dying at any second.

Unless he did something. Anything. But his foolish human brain was slow to respond. It clung desperately to what it thought was safe and infallible. He stubbornly kept thinking, "This should never have happened. This was not supposed to happen..."

BUT IT DID HAPPEN. Patsy Bitterman looked up from her paperback and gazed out over the deep, deep, eternal blue of a southern sea. She wasn't even sure what had happened. All of a sudden, here she was, completely free, supposedly relaxing on a gorgeous beach in Mexico. She sighed and for a minute felt totally jet-lagged – too exhausted by the heat and humidity to shift her miserable beached body. Thank goodness for . . . what was her name? It sounded like Thea, and she said she was twelve years old. Anyway, thank goodness for a twelve-year-old stranger who picked her up and stayed by her side for cheap.

Patsy's decision to take her leave of a bad situation at home was impulsive. To be or not to be in Mexico. It took her breath away.

"Whatever you want, I get. OK, *señora,*" the little girl with the shockingly hard face, which she hid with an accomplished smile, kept reminding Patsy in her service-sector english.

Patsy was a sucker for anyone who said that to her. The nice motherly woman at the travel agency had said the same thing, exactly when Patsy needed an out. And then she'd fixed it all up on her computer, just like that, crooning all the while about how much Patsy needed and deserved her dream getaway.

The best part of the dream getaway was when Patsy told Susan. Her ex-girlfriend had actually sagged, wrinkling like the stretch marks on her ass. It was, of course, the last thing Susan had expected when she came back to retrieve more of her stuff from their home. She slumped over a chair, her brown eyes miraculously brimming with tears, and said, "You play such awful games, Patsy."

Hah, she should talk, Patsy thought. But she had thoroughly prepared her little announcement, and without so much as a quaver in her voice, she replied, "I am not playing games, Susan."

At the back of her mind, Patsy kept harbouring this warm and fuzzy fantasy that Susan would break down, say that she was sorry and beg to come back to her because she still loved her. And they would be the way they used to be. Uncomplicated. Meaningfully attached. Cosy little vacations for two. Dinners with wine. Sharing the bill.

Unfortunately Patsy couldn't bring herself to ask Susan for

anything any more. She was too mindful of the argument that would probably ensue despite their best controls.

"Patsy, you know I can't afford it. Why are you doing this?"

Wasn't it just like Susan to suspect her motives.

"Why do you have to cross-examine everything?" Patsy once shot back at Susan after she had asked why Patsy seemed to have relationships only with women of colour. Patsy disliked answering questions – any questions, and not this irritating one especially. How much of this personal-is-political crap can one take anyway, she thought. And Susan had the distinct tendency to lob these questions at her whenever she was most relaxed and unsuspecting, like so many terrorist grenades into her bed or bathtub or wineglass.

"Did you know that obsessive reading is a sign of unresolved anger?" asked Susan playfully. At that time she was irresistibly nude and brown all over, straddling Patsy's belly on a private wharf at the deserted end of a quiet lake somewhere. She had a fistful of the season's first plump blueberries, which she was try-ing to poke individually into every orifice and crevice she could find on Patsy – not the least of which was her very interested big mouth, so thank goodness she didn't have to answer that one seriously.

"While it's true that some dykes are quite celebrated for their challenging of male privilege, others basically want to take obvi-ous male privileges for themselves, and to me this is dangerously misogynist, don't you think?" Susan gushed like a sunbeam, as she stood high up on an aluminium ladder in the pouring rain, after passing up bundles of shingles to Patsy, who was at the end of her sopping wet rope, trying to finish up a roof that she had stupidly contracted at a financial loss to herself. That time Patsy slammed down the bundle with a loud bang, went up one side of Susan and down the other for being so completely off the wall. Susan's point, of course, got lost in the scuffle.

"Patsy, how many people do you know who don't have a pornographic sense of themselves?" There she went again. And right after Patsy had made up with her and was blissfully closing her eyes for the night with Susan lovingly tucked in her arms like a furry toy. She was a perfect fit, and Patsy loved the smell of her, so she decided to ignore that one.

"I don't cross-examine everything. Just you," retorted Susan blithely, getting up and dressed. About to take off, after pressing all the wrong buttons. After they were already nicely snuggled up in bed together. Patsy felt she started these mind games on purpose, and responded likewise, until Susan waved her little white flag.

"I was just kidding, OK? Don't tie your tits in a knot. And let go of my arm, please," she asked nicely.

Patsy used to laugh uproariously at Susan's apparently witless ways of lampooning her redneck expressions, but more and more lately Patsy felt stung, as if she had been punched out by words. They were just words, and Susan usually felt bad afterward. At which point she'd come back to bed, plying Patsy with soothing remarks, until Patsy felt better. Susan, or so Patsy thought, seemed different from all the others. She had her head screwed on right.

"*Comida, señora?*" Thea asked, jolting Patsy back to the beach, where she realized that it was getting dark, her bum was numb and her stomach growling. The beach was quite emptied of its tourist-mites. Now, even the urchin beside her was getting restless.

Unfortunately, she thought, *comida* was going to be a bit of a problem. Earlier today the hotel had found out that she was over her credit-card limit. There was a big tadoo mexican stink about it. Well, she managed to straighten that mess out and finally convinced them not to turf her out. However, she'd be damned if she'd eat in one of their hoity-toity restaurants ever again. She knew that she would probably land up at Castro's, the local bar and grill. She wasn't looking forward to it, not so much because of the memories, but because the scene was so much grittier there. Cash only. Food was secondary. And she'd have to play along with the creepy barflies. The lack of money had definitely put a damper on her well-deserved vacation.

What the heck! She needed a drink more anyway. She was going to be OK. Just fine and dandy. She had already wired Louise for money. Good old Louise, her old standby – she'd spring her. No matter what, they had a code of loyalty by which they always measured lovership and friendship.

Then who should come to mind again except Susan, who had once openly declared, "Don't ask me for loyalty, Patsy. I don't understand it. I am suspicious of its white-boys'-club implications. Patsy, why don't you just tell me honestly what you really want from me? OK, honey?"

Not only was that Patsy's first shocking surprise about Susan but her biggest mistake in their whole relationship. Anybody who doesn't understand loyalty should have been a total and immediate write-off. But at the time Patsy really wanted to connect with this woman, so she tried to explain what she meant. And Susan tried to explain what she meant. Now, come to think of it, Patsy can't remember if they ever resolved this issue. Fine time to realize that, eh? When Patsy would rather die than ask Susan for help. Best of all, she knew Susan would be very hurt by this.

But five years down the drain also hurt Patsy. Susan called it quits, right out of the blue. That was what upset Patsy the most. She just axed the whole relationship in one fell swoop. OK, Patsy had tried to negotiate. If Susan wanted to go back to school, they could have lived apart. They had done that before. But, no, Susan did not want a relationship at all.

"No, Patsy. That's not what I said. If you would only drop the defences, I actually said that our relationship will have to change, or we'll have no relationship at all," Susan patiently reminded her again, as they both soaked up the sun on the back porch, with their cups of coffee steaming in the cool morning air. The last of those fresh and lovely spring days together.

"Five years down the tube – just like that!" repeated Patsy stubbornly, after yet another upset with Susan, when she drove her beat-up old clunker hard and fast along familiar roads on a moonless night. She remembered that she only had one headlight left, but she was going to follow it religiously, even if it killed her.

As luck would have it, at Castro's bar and grill, the owner and waiters recognized her. Patsy sat in the middle of the crowded room and smiled at them as nicely as she could, while they watched her warily. None of them had changed in five years. They still sold margueritas made with fresh lime by the jugful. Patsy waved a waiter over. The owner called his wife out of the kitchen to serve her. Patsy was in fact amused at this special treatment. It told her that he remembered the incident that involved Susan, Louise and herself in his establishment.

After she had her third drink, Patsy thought about how optimistic she and Susan had been at the beginning – even their first disagreement felt like an engaging part of the process of getting to know each other. It was a heated discussion in which Susan accused Patsy of manipulating Louise. Actually she said, "poor, pitiful Louise."

"That's ridiculous." Patsy recalled her own staunch defence: "Louise is a grown woman. And she is totally responsible for her own stuff."

Not everybody can vacation with her ex-lover and her new lover at the same time, but it wasn't as if Patsy had purposely planned it like that. Louise had insisted that she was going to be there at the same time because she wasn't able to change any of her bookings. And it was true that Patsy and Louise had originally planned that trip together, before Susan came into the picture. And it is a very small resort town, so it would have been very difficult to avoid each other. Thank goddess, Susan didn't seem to mind Louise at all. In fact, they even did stuff together, like two little piggies going to market.

OK, maybe Louise was a bit "possessive," as Susan put it. And a little upset as well, kicking up a bunch of dust trying to prove she wasn't. In other words, she had some unresolved emotional stuff. But what could Patsy do about that? She was totally into Susan by then.

And how could Patsy have known that Louise would act out the way she had – over a jug of cactus-and-lime juice, and with such drastic consequences? And wasn't it the stupidest situation ever to begin with – every tom, dick and hairy category of tourist you can imagine, under the influence of who knew what shit, in a tacky lowlife mexican bar?

"Patsy, you set her up," concluded Susan, quite unfairly, Patsy thought. It was getting so that Patsy couldn't tell her any-thing. Wasn't it obvious that Patsy didn't have any control over that disgusting strip show that had started everything? If Susan was such a know-it-all, why hadn't she gotten them all out while they still had the chance?

"How the hell could I have known that it would turn into such a fiasco? At first, I thought it would be an interesting cul-tural experience. And we were hungry. We had ordered food, which never did come, and Louise had popped up and fetched another jug," recited Susan, "but in retrospect, we should have all known better. Het sex has all the licence, doesn't it? We don't have any. You can't fight that kind of thing and win."

Whenever Susan starts to talk like that, Patsy feels like soak-ing her head, which was already disconnected from her body, in a toilet. Susan likes to call herself a relentless thinker, but to Patsy what she thought was unrepentant nonsense, plain and simple. And she always missed the point – so busy playing Scrabble with that hoity-toity vocabulary of hers – frequently whacking Patsy about the ears with her random misfiring.

What happened at the bar was this. The three of them had quite successfully formed a tight enough huddle against the teeming drunks who surrounded them and sniffed for a way in through their legs. The more obnoxious ones got a resounding "Fuck off" from Patsy or Louise. After a while, all three began to laugh, and enjoy themselves.

Susan was elated with the tasteful silver-and-turquoise ring Patsy had bought for her. And Patsy loved watching her all flushed and lovely and was quite unabashedly feeding off her exhilaration. They were fluttering around each other like Walt Disney butterflies.

Louise had left the table abruptly, squeezed her way back with another jugful and excitedly pointed out another group of women she had found. They were five of them, clearly ameri-can because they were so waving friendly, and very intent on joining forces. Louise really wanted to meet them, and it did make sense to join them if only because their table was closer to the tiny stage and had more breathing space. They were a raunchy, jovial bunch, and Patsy and Louise would have nor-mally fit right in, but they didn't know what to do with Susan, who immediately became standoffish.

Later Susan would claim that they provided Patsy with an audience. This offended Patsy even more. Patsy saw things so differently. She did remember that she was feeling very erotic at the time. And in the safety of a large group of women ("White women," interrupted Susan with a sniff. "Whatever," growled Patsy, struggling for control of her temper), it was easier to show her intense affection towards Susan. After all, Patsy would have hated it if she felt left out. So what if her attentive caresses got a lot of leering, sneering and jeering male attention.

"I mean, fuck 'em!" exclaimed Patsy emphatically. •

Suddenly the overhead lights, already bleary and dim, disappeared, and strobe lights came on and shocked them silly. Hump music, as Louise referred to it, boomed away conversation, half-intelligent or not. The crowd whistled and cheered as a young girl, her face made spiky with caked-on mascara, came on stage and did vulgar bitch-in-heat kinds of poises. Her body was thin and dark and underaged, her mind not there, only the simper about her mouth. She did the mechanical bumps and grinds, the contortions, the usual locomotion until another woman popped out onstage. This one was older, though certainly not old, and fleshier, definitely more into lighting up the world with her star qualities. The audience was, of course, manipulated into a lusty enthusiasm.

Patsy was disgusted and was thoroughly into expressing it. So what if she upset a few of the burly creeps around them. She actually stood up while the little stripper was on her back, on the floor, at her most enthralling moment of curling over and reaching for her cunt, still tastefully g-stringed and sequined, with her tiny wet pink tongue. And yelled out, "Little girl, you are very beautiful, but you're too young. They can't pay you enough for this. You remember that. *You are very beautiful . . .* "

Susan had to yank Patsy back down to her place, because she was getting cat-called out of existence, and Susan was beginning to worry for their safety. Patsy was hell-bent on disrupting the men's mood. ("And we should all know better than to disrupt men's moods," scoffed Patsy years later.)

Then Louise got right into the spirit of things. She didn't look up, but she called out, "A nice girl like you should be in college." The american women kind of shrank away from Patsy and Louise and Susan.

Susan, who was also a bit half-cut, felt compelled to lean over and correct her. "Louise, dear, that's so condescending.

How do you know she's not in college already? You should watch those north american assumptions, you know."

Louise looked somewhat taken aback. But she did shut up. Then, if only because the starlets on stage were making out with each other, everyone quietened and watched one woman hold the other woman's breasts up to the audience for show-and-tell.

But wouldn't you know it, quick as a saucy wink, a man had to step in. And with a big black rubber prick erected on for comic relief. And an evil-looking leather thong strapped about his fist for intrigue.

Uh-oh. That got Patsy all up in irate arms, her eyes wicked and wrathful. But she was amazingly calm, and all she said un-der her breath was something like, if that guy so much as lifts a finger against any one of those women . . . She meant that she was not going to sit around and watch violence being done to women. Sure enough, the guy unravelled the snake and started to make threatening moves – obviously, or why else would he have it up there to begin with? – and Patsy poised herself to strike. But before anybody realized what was happening, Louise had scaled table and chairs with breathtaking agility, jumped up on the stage, grabbed the offensive symbol out of his hands, thrown it down in disgust and stomped it as dramatically dead as the patriarchy itself. The guy was so surprised that he just stood there, dangling his doodoo, his mouth hanging open.

Suddenly four assholes jumped Louise, followed by six more from nowhere. In fact, the whole damn place seemed to con-verge on her. Patsy leaped up and got right into the fray, shov-ing and pushing and trying to reach Louise, who was taking blows but basically still standing.

Susan screeched, "Somebody, help her," at the other women, who were pretty hefty and athletic, but they sat there all numbed out.

Thank goodness the waiters and bouncers got up and helped drag off Louise's attackers. Even the nude dancers tried to fend them off; otherwise, she would have been flattened for good. After a while, it was impossible to see if she was dead or alive, for all the heaving bodies and flailing arms.

The most decisive move, however, came from the naked dancers, wouldn't you know it? Tired of getting their boobs slopped back and forth, the two women began to yell over and over again, "*Cervezas gratis. Cervezas gratis,*" which Patsy understood all right, but didn't comprehend at the time. In an instant, she noticed that the snarls and shoves seemed to lose oomph. And the owner didn't miss a choreographed beat either.

"*Cervezas para todos,*" he kept saying, making gestures of calm. "*Nada. Aqui no ha pasado – nada!*"

Before Patsy had figured it out, the boys were patting each other on the back, all palsy-walsy again, and there was poor Louise, sprawled on the platform, stunned silly, staring at the strobe lights. Susan had sat her up too suddenly, and though she grinned stupidly, she moaned and tipped over again.

"I paid," complained Patsy over the years. "Didn't I pay? The beer should have been on the goddamn house. Why did I have to pay for their bloody free beer?"

"Didn't you get it? If you hadn't, you would have gotten us all beaten up again," followed Susan, ever faithful to her cause, right on cue. "As it was, you came pretty close."

"Well, of all the bloody stupid situations. I wasn't going to pay for their beer. It was like paying to get beat up," retorted Patsy.

"No, paying to not get beat up was more like it, and that, my dear, is the het lifestyle for us women especially," said Susan decisively.

Louise's collar bone had been snapped in two. It was an awful mess. She lay in her hotel room, cradled her arm and cried like a baby for three whole days. And refused drugs. If it had been Patsy, she would have put herself on a ten-day stone, high, acid trip, and no less. Louise looked so terribly bruised and wretched. It was difficult for Patsy to hang around and watch.

The romantic holiday was ruined. And for the rest of the time there, Susan mostly hung about Louise's hotel room, writing, forever writing in that blasted journal of hers in that chirpy way of hers, on the breezy balcony. Who knows what she records in there. She went shopping for fruits and drinks and snacks, made instant coffee for Louise and had dinners in the hotel with Patsy. She didn't want to go out, always complaining that the sun was too yang or something like that.

Suddenly Patsy jerked awake and looked around in disbelief. She couldn't have passed out and spent the night right here on an unwiped table in a forlorn little bar. The mexican bartender stared impassively at her. She was quite alone. Even Thea, or whatever her name was, had gone. Oh shit, and so, of course, had her wallet.

As a result, later that morning, she had to stagger all the hot and dusty way to the American Express office, where, hopefully, rescue from Louise waited for her.

"Dear Patsy," Louise's letter began tentatively at first.

You know — or even if you don't — I've changed. Hey, I've had to. I was in so much pain, I basically didn't have any choice.

Last night, after your telegram, I spent some time thinking about me and you, and do you know what? I remembered that you and I are old friends first. We've come through a lot of shit together. When you get back, we need to sit down and have a good honest talk. It's been a while since I've seen you, but I've been wanting to tell you about some of the growing up that I have been doing on my own.

I really want to help you, except for one very important thing.

And believe me, just sending you the money you need is a lot eas-
ier than not sending it. I feel the best way I can help you, and I
wish someone was compassionate enough to do the same thing for
me at the time of my pain, is to turn on all the lights so that you
can take a good look at yourself. Please listen to me, Patsy. When
that happened to me, I saw something that amazed me. There is
no audience out there. Never has been one. I was basically up on
that stage all by myself, screaming and bawling and acting out to
nobody. Then, in spite of the blow to my fragile ego, sooner or
later I did what I had to do – pick myself up and crawl off. Do
you know what I mean at all? This doesn't mean that I don't love
you, because I do love you very much. And I really hope that I'll
see you very soon.
Louise

When Patsy looked up at the glaring tropical sun, she realized
that she had lost her sunglasses and sunscreen as well. She
thought she saw Thea down the street, or someone who looked
like a dark, thin, shadowy girl in a dingy T and faded pink cotton pants, who followed an older heavier white woman, who
looked like an north american tourist alone. And she also realized. Of course. A street-smart kid like her would be able to
smell flat-out stone-broke a mile away. She knew better than to
hang about bathetically.

But Patsy didn't know what to do. On impulse she opened
up her paperback to read:

Errol Spiridigliozzi's heart thumped like a savage drum in his
throat. He felt sick as he clung fearfully to the narrow icy ledge of
this remote mountain, the fierce winds tearing and nipping at his
legs, threatening to throw him off balance. On one horrid stretch
where some parts were so narrow and precarious, and other parts
had broken away, his feet refused to move. His hands, tortured

and frozen, gripped the rock face. Panting and gasping for breath, he ever so painfully, slowly inched towards the windy point of cliff beyond him.

$\mathcal{L}$ESBIANS AND OTHER SUBVERSIVES

TERESA TOYOTA IS NOT ONLY Naomi's escape route, but her shell of protection as well. No wonder her hand lingers on the door handle after she has locked the car. Who else loves their subcompact enough to name her after a TV newscaster who reminds her of an electronic geisha doll in a Sony glass box?

Upon turning, she spots them at four hundred yards – three lovely blond teenagers in school uniforms waiting at the entrance, eager to extend their hospitality. Naomi tosses her waist-length black hair back and steps forward to meet them halfway. Wide smiles all around, like wreaths of laurel on windswept golden hair. Pink-ankled muses, nymphs in their pagan pastoral setting. In ancient knowledge; in splintered sunlight. Hand in hand, in tender dance.

Inside the all-girls catholic school, Naomi sits down to tea with the guidance counsellor, Ms. Flannigan, and fifteen fresh faces. Naomi shakes hands with every one of them, like the true ambassador she is. She notes that a good half of the class cannot meet her steadfast gaze. The girls apparently prepare a tea every week. Speakers are invited to come.

"So I guess that's how we got onto the subject of women's studies. Of course, many of our girls expressed an interest in the women's studies program at the university," says Ms.

Flannigan, with Royal Doulton raised to her lips, cool as a cucumber sandwich. Her eyes are incredibly intense and she watches Naomi as carefully as Naomi watches her. Ms. Flannigan, sipping hot water, continues, "I have a friend who teaches there. And she has been guiding the girls through a mini-introductory course, so to speak. She was very enthusiastic about our idea of having a member of the Beyond Borders collective come and speak to us. Although she doesn't personally know your group, she has heard of your work. In fact, to be quite frank, she was as interested in learning about your collective's work as we are."

As Naomi listens, a charming little one comes close and offers her a selection of cakes.

"Do try the fruitcake, Ms. Suzuki. We make it in bake shop. It has become quite a school tradition."

Naomi obliges as giggles tinkle through the medieval air of the lounge. Late-afternoon sun streaks in through the tall gothic windows, lighting up the huge stone fireplace with its incised latin motto *Ad Lucem.* Well-worn, well-made armchairs, doilies, plants, linen, silver, tea and sweets – all these niceties warm Naomi into a state of stupor.

"Then your friend recommended Beyond Borders to you?" Naomi sits up a little.

"No, my dear. Here is where I shall reintroduce Melanie to you."

Does Naomi imagine it or has Ms. Flannigan's smile the slightest edge to it?

"This is Melanie's idea, after all; she arranged this tea, and she is your official hostess. Melanie?"

Melanie is the centrepiece of the room, one of the trio who welcomed Naomi so warmly.

Melanie stands up to another bout of giggling and meaningful glancing about. Slipping a piece of paper into her uniform's pocket, she folds her hands modestly in front of her, as if over her most vulnerable spot.

"Ms. Suzuki," Melanie begins her practised speech, "welcome again to Seton Academy. We very much appreciate your driving a good distance from Lantzville to talk to us." She hesitates, and the roomful of girls quietens.

"I want to say that I am very nervous." Melanie's green eyes glue on to the face of her almost twinlike companion, whose name Naomi has forgotten. "Although today's topic is mostly my idea, lots of girls had to fight . . . work very, very hard to prepare this forum for your ideas, Ms. Suzuki. This is only about half the class. Many girls couldn't come . . ."

Off to Naomi's side, there is a half-drawn breath from Ms. Flannigan, who sits stock-still.

"I guess I have to say that I'm really disappointed at the lack of support," Melanie goes on. "I felt that after the quality of education we have received, we should be more able to think for ourselves. As Mother Superior said, in another few months we will all be graduated and on our own. All along she has encouraged us to be open to new ideas. And in the end she refused to censor us. I never . . . I guess I never realized how much we censor ourselves, though . . . with our own fears."

The more Melanie speaks, the more visibly upset she becomes, her body tense and poised on the edge. Is she about to cry? Naomi closes her eyes to imagine what it is to be Melanie, to be privileged, to grow up with arrogant impunity within straight and narrow parameters. Melanie has the confidence of a natural leader because she has always been indulged. Now she has come face to face with stinging rejection for the first time in her young life.

Aah, this picture puzzle is piecing itself together very nicely, thinks Naomi. They all do in the end. She is used to the panting, cried-out women; their histrionics are often exhausted long before she has the chance to open her mouth. Three years ago, when Naomi first agreed to take on this project, her collective friends and intimates reacted much the same way – from bad and barbed jokes to impacted hysteria at such an absurd notion as giving educational talks on being a lesbian to schoolgirls. Ridiculous. At the time, Naomi couldn't explain her motives except to say that big picture puzzles were her favourite pastime. The more intricate and complex, the better.

Even so, Naomi is beginning to get a little worried. She glances at her watch. One half hour, and the word *lesbian* has not passed anyone's lips, not even her own. Each situation is different, and this one with its smooth porcelain engineering makes her feel like an invisible germ soon to be swooshed down a sanitized drain. Time to begin the swim against the current; she has at most forty minutes left to explain – excuse her, suggest – an explanation for the most essential split in power ever devised by humankind. But there is Melanie still snuffling on and on about how white middle-class liberalism has just failed her.

Naomi shyly, slyly puts up her hand. When everyone's attention finally, reluctantly shifts her way, she asks, "Perhaps if you will allow me, I can make a few suggestions . . . " Then, as Naomi has always done, she openly declares herself: "I am a lesbian. I came here to tell you, if you are willing to listen, about myself and my community. I am also here to learn about you and . . ." And each word follows the other in a calming, charming, orderly fashion.

What Naomi fails to mention, as she always does, is that she thinks of everyone as lesbians. Some know it, some come to know it, and some, as lesbian writer Audre Lorde said, will die stupid. This is the secret of how she is able to talk to them so gently; this is how she diffuses the hate and the anger – the fear being the hardest to reach. But she never thinks of herself as lesbian on their terms – what would she ever be but the poor, oppressed minority forever and ever? Amen! Instead she thinks about everybody on her terms, on her own turf, so to speak. They are quite simply no different from her and doesn't that make them all lesbians. She is not exclusionist. *Un fait accompli!*

"What exactly is a lesbian?" Mrs. Flossie Bell had asked point-blank; with her, two other wizened old faces pushed up against Naomi, who three years ago looked exactly as she does now, with a wide-open square face, a stockade body and a magnificent headful of jet-black hair. Naomi had been building a shrimp-and-avocado sandwich on a tea towel at Beyond Borders' front counter, and was well aware of how many times Mrs. Bell's ancient black Caddy had cruised by their bookstore before it parked. A total of seven times. Lantzville is her hometown, and she knew that the car was not local. The first hungry bite into the food of goddesses and she was in heaven. She couldn't even bring herself to be annoyed by the presence of Mrs. Bell and the two other prissy old ladies who wheezed into the store and clattered about the bookshelves with much stilted fuss and ado.

"To me," replied Naomi with careful composure, "a lesbian is a person who does not have her beauty defined by the male order any more." She did not bat an eyelash. No one could accuse her of not having a sense of humour.

The one named Flossie Bell stared at her for a dumbfounded minute. Then she opened her clip-top purse, reached into one of its panels for her bifocals and what Naomi immediately recognized to be the application form that she and Rocky had painstakingly toiled over for weeks. It requested grant money from the Carter Foundation to start an information and library-exchange network to service fifteen women's shelters and centres in ten rural townships.

Their application had been turned down by the foundation, said Mrs. Flossie Bell, but it had been handpicked from among the rejects for consideration by their group, the Knights of Turf, with herself as secretary/treasurer, Mrs. Moira McAteer as acting steward, and Mrs. Studs Ryan as acting grand marshall.

"We like your community project idea, and we are looking for possible recipients of the charitable monies we have made available through our organization," she declared, causing Naomi's mouth to go slack with sheer amazement, which happened rarely.

Two weeks after that, stoned on margueritas beside the late Mr. Studs Ryan's oceanview pool, Naomi's lips, puckered from the salty lime, formed the words, "Oh, come on, Malu, the idea's so outrageous, I can't resist it!"

Marilou P., sworn off alcohol, retorted, "It's a setup. I know it. I've been a victim too long. It's too good."

Stoned on reefer, Flossie Bell and Moira McAteer looked like melted-down grannies. The rest of the Beyond Borders collective had taken this very rare opportunity to chase each other around or into the chevron-shaped pool. Wet heads bopped merrily in the water. Rocky screeched, "Wait. Let me at least take off my jeans!" Mrs. Ryan lovingly marinaded thick red meat on the barbecue.

The Knights of Turf had been established as a social club in 1938 and in its heyday had attained a membership of five hundred and fourteen. But now there were just the four of them, including a Mrs. Saintfield Melvihill, who had been jailed in a care facility after a massive stroke, her power of attorney lost to three ungrateful wretches of sons. Mrs. McAteer added to this part of the telling, "We really learned the meaning of 'you can't take it with you.'"

Naomi had begun to see individual traits surface out of these women's pale-blue-tinted hairdos. Moira was flat and tough.

Her anger made her eyes sleepy and her cheeks sallow. Flossie was stocky and solid, energetic and boisterous. Mrs. Ryan was terribly stressed out. Whenever Saintfield Melvihill was mentioned, which was often, Moira and Flossie always looked cautiously over to Mrs. Ryan, who bustled about even faster. Food and drinks and towels for the girls! She seemed to be near her breaking point, but how can a stranger tell for sure.

"There're just the three of us now. We are it. We are the Knights of Turf . . . " A split second to consider this, and suddenly the ladies burst open into hysterical laughter, splitting their sides.

" . . . all dressed up and nowhere to go." They laughed even harder as they told their story.

The Knights of Turf had total assets of $4.2 million — most of it in a lovely run-down brick 1949 building on the west side of Vancouver. Consistently a fun-loving group, the Knights of Turf had not always been its name. It started as a wartime dance club. Back then, whenever the gals ran out of dance partners, they went out and got some more. They were not the types to worry about names and such, until the postwar period when the men came back, claimed ownership of the club and named it the Knights of Epithius. The club eventually petered out, with no new blood. The members grew old and staunch together. Their children grew up and away. The core group stayed a consistent bridge neat sixteen for decades, with a call-back community of fifty or so. One year, 1967, they boasted one hundred at their annual Robbie Burns banquet.

They were not liberal, so they had no liberal guilt. Their good ol' boys club was as exclusive and pompous and as truculent as they pleased. Their favourite after-dinner activity was making loud verbal assaults on the government, who were a bunch of commies and chink-lovers. (That year was 1957, and the newly elected Member of Parliament was Douglas Jung.

And, oh yes, the Scotch was Piper's, 1934.) The girls were the ones who answered the revenue letters addressed "Dear Sirs." They paid for the hired help; they sent for the crates of whiskey; they stuffed and they decorated, and in the end they braced the falling-down columns until, finally, they fell down.

Naomi and Marilou accepted the Knights of Turf donation. Ever since then, their collective has made wonderful use of the grant money, which appeared in their bank account on March 8 every year for the past three, the empty boys' clubhouse having transformed itself into crowded pink tiers of upscale boutiques and offices and condominiums. The "Knives" of Turf went into seclusion after Saintfield passed away. However, Naomi wonders how seclusive they are since she has had a steady stream of requests for speaking engagements right from the start and from the weirdest places. An inner-city high school next week, a class of nursing students a month ago.

Word of mouth, especially old women's mouths, gets around, Naomi thinks, making her way back to Teresa Toyota.

Melanie has been left hanging, but, from the perplexed look on her face, Naomi suspects that at least she is beginning to know that she is hanging, and after that it will simply be a matter of whether she wants to remain like that, and for how long. She seemed a determined sort of girl. Naomi's last polite glimpse of Ms. Flannigan revealed a woman askew, as if she was leaving a doctor's office and wondering at the slickness of the procedure.

"Giddyup, Teresa!" Naomi murmurs softly, her seed sown to grow up tall and slender. Grass swaying against big open sky. She looks left, right, rear and in front of her. Mainstream, she tells herself at the entrance of the highway, merging with a smile.

She sees herself going into the city next week, into their prisonlike high schools. Their men, like terrorists, at the back of the classroom, eyes lined with bootblack, long savage hair, fashion accessories like weapons. In spite of appearances, they are riot police, there hoping that someone will get out of hand. And their women with brooding faces and pitiful slim hands, herded into the centre of the room, where they can be watched, come to watch Naomi's execution. They all know the importance of gesture. Any young child does. If she is allowed to be, then why can't they? This challenge will be intolerable to their men. But still Naomi knows that someone in their midst was willing to risk the fuckin'-dyke-hate-men-willya fist exploding her nose. And that alone is enough for her. And her presence alone there can also often be enough.

So she takes her time. Always a careful driver, she buggies Teresa along slowly towards a future of her own quiet making.

BOB HSIANG

SKY LEE is a feminist writer and artist, and author of *Disappearing Moon Cafe*, a 1990 finalist for the Governor General's Literary Award in Canada and winner of the Vancouver Book Award. She is co-editor of *Telling It: Women and Language Across Cultures* and illustrator of the children's book, *Teach Me How to Fly, Skyfighter.*

Born in Port Alberni, British Columbia, Lee holds a Bachelor of Fine Arts Degree from the University of British Columbia, as well as a Diploma in Nursing from Douglas College. She lives on the West Coast with her son, Nathan.

PRESS GANG PUBLISHERS FEMINIST CO-OPERATIVE is committed to producing quality books with social and literary merit. We give priority to Canadian women's work and include writing by lesbians and by women from diverse cultural and class backgrounds. Our list features vital and provocative fiction, poetry and non-fiction.

A free catalogue is available from Press Gang Publishers, 101- 225 East 17th Avenue, Vancouver, B.C. V5V 1A6 Canada